Enjoy!

MW01274269

# EXPLORING
## JUST BECAME
# REAL

Karen Hillier

 FriesenPress

One Printers Way
Altona, MB R0G 0B0
Canada

www.friesenpress.com

**Copyright © 2022 by Karen Hillier**
First Edition — 2022

All rights reserved.

ISBN
978-1-03-915626-5 (Hardcover)
978-1-03-915625-8 (Paperback)
978-1-03-915627-2 (eBook)

1. *FICTION, CRIME*

Distributed to the trade by The Ingram Book Company

# Dedication

I dedicate this book to my two daughters, Krystal and Kayla, who are always there to encourage me to keep going. (Never give up, Mom. You got this.)

In memory of my dad, Ernest W Burke. July 10, 1931- October 17, 2017, whom I miss dearly. Life is not the same without you, Pops.

# Introduction

Living in the woods in a cabin can have many things happen. There is nothing better to do except explore and go on adventures. When you go to a farmhouse and find a bucket full of human hands. Well, that's a little creepy for the mind. All the men who have been tortured in a barn as you see the chains and handcuffs dangling from a ceiling post. A young man tied to a tree and tortured to death. You then come to find an infant body in a small wooden chest as you see a pink blanket sticking out. Who in their right mind could do this? you say, as you must get outside for air. So much is wrong in this world we live in. Trying to get young teenage girls off the streets and out of the prostituting ring. Life is full of surprises. Exploring and adventures. Well, you never know what you will find. It just makes you crave more.

Karen A. Hillier

**IT WAS A BEAUTIFUL** sunny July morning. I could hear the squealing tires on the highway as I headed outside to have my morning coffee on my deck. It sounded like there had been an accident not far from my little cabin in the woods. As I sat outside and listened to the birds chirping, I could hear an ambulance in the distance. I decided to get dressed and head down the highway to see what had happened. As I made my way to my car, I could hear more sirens. I headed down my long, narrow driveway to head to the accident. I wasn't sure what to expect but wanted to go in case I could be of some help.

As I got closer to the accident, I saw a red car rolled over in the ditch. The police had the road blocked off and the ambulance was on scene. I got out of my car and walked toward the police car that was parked on the side of the road. As I got closer, I saw Officer Burns, whom I recognized, standing there taking notes from another driver. I waited until he was done talking and went over to see what had happened. We said hi to each other and Officer Burns told me what happened.

The witness said she had been driving behind the little red car when it suddenly veered off the road. She could see the driver on the phone and it looked like she was texting. Her head was going up and down and then suddenly she hit the dirt, and her car flipped. It all happened so fast. She stopped and checked on her but couldn't get her out. She called an ambulance and the police.

The girl was finally out of the car and put in the ambulance. I could tell she was hurt by all the blood. She had a neck brace on, and she was out on a back board. The sirens were on and away the ambulance went. Officer Burns was handed her purse so he could get some ID. He needed to contact her family and let them know about the accident.

The traffic started to move again, and the little red car stayed in the ditch. A tow truck would soon be on the way to get it out of there. Accidents can happen so quickly, and she was lucky to be alive.

Officer Burns was helping me to take courses to be able to work with the police. I would need to take an undercover course and a self-defence course. I'd worked briefly with Officer Burns and his team over the last year. I'd helped them solve many cases involving criminals.

I went over to say goodbye to Officer Burns, and he said he would call me the next day. "We have two courses for you to take," he said. "One is a three-month day course, and the other is a night course. We would like you to finish these courses to be able to work with us. I will call you tomorrow with all the details on them."

I said, "I look forward to your phone call."

I went to my car and headed home to enjoy the rest of my day. I put the windows down and let the air blow through as I listened to my country music. After a few minutes, I headed up my driveway. I was planning to go for a walk after lunch. I sat on the deck for about a half hour before I went inside the cabin. It was such a beautiful sunny day, and the smell of the flowers was breathtaking.

My phone rang and it was Officer Burns. The girl in the accident had been following a blue truck that had just kidnapped her sister. She was on the phone with her brother at the time, when suddenly she lost control and went in the ditch. She gave her brother the description and the partial licence plate of the truck. She said they were at the mall shopping when they were approached by two guys. One of the guys, who had a dark complexion, asked the girls for direction to a place they had never heard of.

As we came out of the mall and headed to our car, we were followed by the blue truck. As we approached my car, one of the guys got out of the truck and grabbed my little sister. She was kicking and screaming as he threw her in the truck and drove off. I quickly got in my car and followed them. I couldn't dial the phone because I didn't want to be distracted and lose sight of the truck. As I was driving, my phone rang, and it was my brother. I told him what happened and where I was. Then, suddenly, my car left the road and went in the ditch. The guy that grabbed her was the guy from the mall who had approached us for directions. He was of dark complexion, 175 pounds, and about 5' 10" tall. He was wearing a grey hoody and jeans. Oh, and he also had on a black baseball cap. The other guy was about the same height but was heavier. I only remember he was wearing a red hoody. Please help find my little sister. She is only fourteen and was screaming for help. We need to find her before they hurt her.

Officer Burns said, "We need to find this truck and we need to find it fast."

I said, "Anything I can do to help, just ask." He gave me the description and license plate of the blue truck and asked me to keep my eye out for it. I told him I would be on the lookout for it and that I hoped we could find the little girl.

After I hung up the phone, I decided to get ready and go for a drive instead of a walk. We needed to find this girl fast or her chances of being found alive were not good. They only had a partial plate but hopefully that would be enough to get the name and address of whoever owned it. At least that would be a start.

I packed a few things in my cooler and headed out the door. I wasn't sure where I was going but thought I would at least drive down a few dirt roads in the area. I knew the area well. I was thinking of the direction they were headed and thought they may not go all the way to town. Maybe, just maybe, they took an off-road and headed down one of the dirt roads.

I drove up and down the roads very slowly, looking for any blue truck I could see. There wasn't much traffic, so it was easy to drive slowly and take my time looking. I came to a white SUV that was stopped on the side of the road. I pulled over and asked them if they'd seen a blue truck in the area. They quickly said "no" and continued taking pictures of the scenery. I thanked them and got back in my car. I continued driving up and down dirt roads for over two hours. I came across another vehicle parked on the side of the road. They were also taking pictures. I got out and asked them if they'd seen a blue truck in the area. They said, "No, but we did see one parked at the end of this road up by an old farmhouse." I thanked them and drove away. I headed in the direction they gave me.

I was hoping this is the truck we were looking for. I drove until I got to the end of the road. There was an old farmhouse with a blue truck parked on the side of it. It looked like the farmhouse had been abandoned for a very long time. The place was boarded up and the roof looked like it was about to cave in. It was in rough shape but at least it was still standing. I tried to get a closer look at the truck, but it was so far away. The driveway was long and narrow. I decided to park my car off to the side and make my way up the driveway. I headed up through the trees so I wouldn't be seen. I walked through the brush and fallen-down trees until I got close enough to get a better look at the truck.

I couldn't see or hear anyone. The door looked like it had been pushed in. The rest of the farmhouse was all boarded up, so I knew they must have kicked or pushed the door in. That would be the only way to get inside. I got close enough to get a few pictures before I called Officer Burns. I wanted to make sure I had the licence plate to see if it was a match to the partial plate they had. Just as I was about to call Officer Burns, I saw one of the guys come out of the house. He had dark skin and was wearing a grey hoody and a black baseball cap. He stood on the step and lit a cigarette. I stayed in the trees and called Officer Burns. I told him where I was and that I'd found the blue truck. I said, "I'm watching one of the guys right now on the step having a cigarette."

He asked me for directions and told me to stay in my car. He told me they were on their way and to stay put. "If they leave, you can follow them and keep me posted," he said. "We need to get this girl home safe."

I didn't go back to my car. I watched from the woods until the guy went back inside the house. I made my way to the blue truck and looked inside. I could see lots of garbage, a rope, and a handgun. I knew these guys were dangerous. I was just hoping they hadn't hurt the girl. I wanted to go to the door and tell them I was having car trouble but knew that wasn't a good idea. I just wanted to get inside so badly to make sure she wasn't hurt.

I waited about thirty minutes until I saw a car coming up the road. I headed to my car to see who it was. It was Officer Burns and his partner. They asked me a few questions and told me to stay at my car. There was another police car coming. After a few minutes, there were six police officers at the scene. They headed up to the farmhouse to surround the house.

After they were all in place, I could hear them say, "The place is surrounded. Come out with your hands up so no one gets hurts." After a minute, one of the guys came out of the house with his hands up. He said, "Don't shoot. I am unarmed, and I surrender." Two of the officers made their way to the step and put him in handcuffs. The officers made their way to the police car and put him in the backseat.

Officer Burns went over to talk to him. "Is the girl hurt? We need to know if the girl is hurt in any way." There was no response from the guy at all. He didn't talk at all.

The officers continued asking the other guy to come out of the house and surrender. One of the officers managed to go around the back of the house and find a board missing on one of the windows. He asked the other officer to find him a ladder or something he could climb on. He wanted to see if he could get a look inside the house. After a few minutes, one of the officers found an old step-ladder laying against a shed. He climbed up and was able to get a look inside of the old farmhouse. He couldn't see much except old furniture that looked like it had been there for many years. He could hear the other guy say, "I'm not giving up. If you want me, you will have to come on and get me. I'm not going back to jail. "

The officers pleaded with him to give up. They said, "No one is hurt. Come out with your hands up before someone gets hurt. We can talk this out. Let the girl go and turn yourself in. It's the only way out."

The guy in the house opened fire and started shooting through a window that was boarded up. He put the gun through a hole in the wood that was over the window. This guy wasn't about to come out without a fight. He wasn't about to give up easily. The officers told him over and over to surrender before someone got hurt. "Let the girl go and we can talk this out." Still nothing. He had no intentions of giving up. We couldn't open fire with the girl inside.

We called in a negotiator to try to talk him out. We knew it was going to be at least a half hour before they got there. We had to continue talking to him so he wouldn't hurt the girl. At this point, we didn't know if the girl was hurt or not. The other guy in the police car wouldn't talk to us.

A police car pulled in to take the guy that surrendered, back to the station. Officer Burns said they were hoping this guy would talk if he was away from the situation. We needed to get information on who we were dealing with. To take him to the station and work on him. We needed to know the name of the guy inside the house. Both men refuse to cooperate. At least we had one in custody. We just needed him to talk.

After a few more minutes, a negotiator arrived on the scene. He introduced himself as Bill. "I am here to help you get out of this situation safe. What is your name? Tell me your name so we can talk this out. I am here to help you. Tell me if the girl is OK." The guy inside would not answer. "Is there anything we can get you? Would you like us to get you some food or drinks?" After a few minutes, there was another shot from the window. Nobody needs to get hurt. Please let the girl go and come out with your hands up."

This went on for another ten minutes. I didn't think this guy had any intention of surrendering. Officer Burns came over and said this guy's name was Devon Smith. He was in prison for ten years and just got out two weeks ago. He was in for armed robbery and attempted murder. He went to prison at the age of twenty. He was in foster care from age six until he was on his own at the age of fifteen. He only knew the street life. He had been bounced from home to home all his life. His parents were drug addicts.

"Devon, we know your situation, so don't make it any worse. Nobody is hurt, so let the girl go. We can talk this through, just let the girl go. She has nothing to do with this. She is just a young girl who is very scared right now. Please don't hurt her. Let her go."

Other officers were around the back of the house trying to get in. Keeping him around the front of the house, talking, would distract him. We were hoping for long enough so we could get someone inside. We still didn't know if the girl was hurt. After another thirty minutes went by, the officer around back finally made his way inside. One by one, the officers were able to get inside without being heard. They needed to assess the situation and make sure the girl was out of the way before they sprang into action and took this guy down.

After a few minutes, we heard another gunshot coming from inside the house. "Suspect is down, suspect is down." That's what we heard over the radio. The team moved in and apprehended the suspect. He was shot, but still alive. They made their way down to a room where the girl was tied to an old metal bed frame. She was alive, but scared. "An ambulance is on the way to take you to get checked over. Everything is going to be OK."

This was a happy ending to a day that could have ended differently. I was so thankful the girl was safe. The suspects were both in custody and this was a happy ending.

Officer Burns came over to thank me. "We wouldn't have found the girl if it wasn't for you. I thank you for all your help in finding her when you did. I am really looking forward to working with you soon. We need you to get these courses done to make this happen. I have all the information in my office. I would like you to stop by tomorrow at 9 a.m., to go over everything and sign the papers. We really need you on our team." We said goodbye and I said, "I will see you tomorrow at 9 a.m."

**I LEFT AND HEADED** home. That had been enough for today. I needed to get home and relax out on my deck. It was a beautiful day with lots of traffic on the highway. I opened my windows and played some country music. I could smell the animals as I drove past the farms in the area. I was close to my driveway when I passed a few people walking on the side of the road. It was a beautiful day for a walk, but I was tired and needed to eat.

I got to the cabin and went inside to make a salad. I had some lettuce and cucumbers cut up. I threw in some chicken and tossed it with French dressing. I added some green peppers and croutons. I grabbed a bottle of cold water and went outside to enjoy the rest of the beautiful sunny day. I sat outside for a few hours. I finished my salad and walked around the property looking at my flowers, which I'd planted. I never did have any luck planting flowers. Sometimes I wondered why I bothered doing it at all. I guess because I hoped, someday, they would surprise me and grow. My friend Lil knew how to plant and get her flowers to grow. I should have taken lessons from her. I cleaned the yard and put some garbage in the fire pit. I would burn it the next day when I got home from town. It was getting late, and I wanted to go inside and relax and watch the news.

I was excited about going to see Officer Burns in the morning, and about getting all the information on the courses I would be taking. These courses were very important and would help me work with the police. I had been waiting a long time to get into these courses. Officer Burns had been waiting a long time, as well, trying to get me in these courses.

After supper, I cleaned up and went outside to sit on my deck with a cup of tea. I looked at the bright blue sky. It didn't get dark until almost 11 p.m. I enjoyed every minute I spent out sitting on my deck. The birds were chirping, and the air was fresh. I could hear the traffic going up and down the highway as I did every evening. I went inside at about 9 p.m., and watched a movie. I opened a couple of windows and let the soft breeze blow through the cabin. It was such a clear night with the sound of the animals echoing inside. It made me relax and have a good night sleep.

I woke up to the sound of birds at about 7 a.m. My windows were still open, and the sun was shining in. I headed out on the deck with a cup of coffee. It was such a peaceful morning. I was excited to meet with Officer Burns so we could go over the courses. It was going to feel weird going back to school.

I finished my coffee and went inside to get ready to head to town. I left my cabin at 8 :30., and headed to the highway. I went through the drive-through for a coffee as I got to town. I went in the station to meet with Officer Burns. I stopped at the front desk to tell her to let Officer Burns know I was there.

I sat in one of the soft leather chairs that were lined up the long, narrow hallway. A few minutes later, Officer Burns came out to greet me. "Let's go to my office where we can talk. Come in and take a seat. I have all the paperwork here for you to read over and sign, when you are finished reading through it. If you have any questions, just ask me. I will leave you alone for about fifteen minutes, and then I will come back and check on you.

I sat and read the stack of papers. There must have been about twenty pages to read over. The papers explained everything I would be learning in the courses I would be taking. There would be undercover work and a self-defence course. The self-defence course would be done at night and the other course would be Monday to Friday from eight to three. They are each three months long and I needed to finish with a 90 percent to be able to work with the police. I knew this was going to be a long three months and lots of studying. I was ready to take this challenge on.

Officer Burns came back in and took a seat. "Do you have any questions before you sign your life away?" "No, everything seems to be straightforward." I signed the papers and handed them to Officer Burns. "You will be busy the next few months. This is what you have been waiting for. This is your chance to get your foot in the door. We need an undercover agent like you. You are just what this department needs. These courses will teach you that safety comes first, and everything is done by the book. The self-defence course is a must and will teach you how to protect yourself when you are out in the field. I will go make you a copy to take with you so you can go over them again at home."

He came back and handed me the copy in a large brown envelope. "You must remember to study as hard as you can and get high marks. There will be eight in your class and twelve in the self-defence class. You will need a notebook, pen, highlighter, and pencil to bring to the class. You can wear comfy clothes and runners to the self-defence class. It's important you show up on time and study every night. Three months will fly by. Have fun and I will be in touch."

I left and headed out to my car. The weather was beautiful, and the sun was hot. I went home and sat on the deck for a couple of hours. I had a few days before I started my courses. I wanted to enjoy my day before I had to spend the next few months studying. I felt like my heart was coming out of my chest I was so happy. I had been waiting for this day for a long time. Nothing made me happier than helping people.

I spent the day cleaning up and thinking about going on an adventure on the weekend. There were so many dirt roads to take and so much to see. I enjoyed going out and exploring different areas. It was so nice to see all the old buildings and farmhouses still standing. Most of the families had moved away or passed away, leaving their property sitting there, falling to the ground. I tried to go inside to just look around to see all the old trinkets. It was amazing to see how our families lived many years ago compared to the world today. There were outhouses and old wood stoves around the yards. I once saw an old well where people would get their water from. They would lower a bucket down on a rope and bring the water up.

I enjoyed my day at home and was enjoying my quiet evening on my deck. My hair was blowing in the breeze and the moon was bright. The sound of the birds chirping was so relaxing. I sat outside for hours, forgetting about the time. I finally went inside at 11 p.m. It was just getting dark. I opened the windows in the cabin and let the wind blow through.

I woke up to the sun shining at about 4 a.m. I knew it was going to be a beautiful day. I fell back asleep until 6 a.m. It was a beautiful sunny day, and the birds were chirping. I made a coffee and went to enjoy the start of my day. I was planning my adventure about where to go. I went inside at 9 a.m., and packed a lunch and grabbed a few bottles of water. After getting dressed, I went out to my car and headed to the highway. I wasn't sure where I was going but knew I would be gone for the day.

I drove for about twenty-five minutes and came to a dirt road. I turned down the road and drove, looking at all the scenery. It was so peaceful and refreshing. My windows were down, and my country music was playing. There wasn't a car in sight. I drove a little farther until I came to a gate at the end of an old farmhouse.

I got out of my car and looked up the long driveway. There was nobody around this old place. It looked like it had been vacant for many years. I decided to walk up the driveway, making my way through the locked gate at the entrance.

As I got closer, I could see most of the windows were boarded up and the door was closed. The roof was full of moss and old, rotted boards. The shingles were all lifted, and the steps were falling apart. I walked up the old, creaky stairs to get to the door. The door was shut, but had no lock on it. I made my way inside to look around. As I entered the old, rickety house, I could see the floors had lifted tiles and holes, so I had to be careful not to fall through the floor. I walked around and down a hallway. There were a couple of bedrooms that had some old furniture in them. One room had an old mattress on the floor.

I made my way to the kitchen. There were a few old chairs that had rips in the seats. They were rusted and the table is upside down. There is an old woodstove in the corner of the kitchen that has a stack of wood beside it. I found a couple of old bottles that were sitting in an open cupboard that had the door hanging off.

I walked around the house, being careful not to fall through the floor. There was no bathroom in the house. I could see an out-house in the backyard. It looked like it was falling apart, and the door was hanging off. I went outside to look around the yard. I went inside a shed that was next to the old outhouse. The door was off the shed and the roof was sagging. I looked around and found some old chains hanging from a rafter. It looked like they might have hung an animal there to dry out. I'm sure, back in the day, that was how they had to eat. They would hunt and survive on the wild animals. I noticed an old wooden box laying against the wall of the shed. The box was large and had a chain wrapped around it. I couldn't see a lock on the chain.

I tried to move the box so I could get the chain off. I pulled and pulled until I could unwrap the chain from around the wooden box. Finally, the chain was off the box. It was heavy and very rusty. I opened the box. I looked through the old, smelly stuff inside. I found clothes and shoes. There was a couple of purses and ladies' watches. I was trying to figure out why this would be there. Who would save this old stuff in a box and put a chain on it? I kept looking until I came across a small black notebook. I opened the book and it had names and dates written in it. I went through it and tried to make sense of what I was reading.

As I flipped through the book, I found a name of a girl on each page. On each page under the girl's name, was a date that said, "Delivery." A little description of each girl and then it had another date at the bottom of the page. I wasn't sure what this meant. I was just hoping this didn't mean these girls were captured and then killed. This didn't make any sense why someone would have these items in a trunk and a notebook with names and dates. It felt creepy and I was scared at what I had just found. I took some pictures of the box and the items in it. I kept the book with me.

I looked around some more and made my way back outside. It was dark in the shed, and I needed some sunlight. I walked around the yard and went to where I'd seen an old, rusted black truck. I walked around the truck and looked inside it. I saw a shovel and some rope and a couple of jackets. The truck had four flat tires and the hood was open. The back of the truck had a pushed-in bumper and it was falling off. The grass was growing tall around the truck and there was a tree over the roof.

I could see a large pile of dirt that had grass and shrubs growing up from it. I continued taking pictures of the area and anything that looked out of the ordinary. I found a few shovels and a couple of old gas cans. This place was starting to give me the creeps.

I walked around and noticed another shed in the distance. As I walked toward it, I could see a wheelbarrow beside it. As I got a little closer, I saw there was a tall green bucket by the opened door. The smell was making me sick to my stomach. There were flies all around the area and swarming the bucket. I lifted the cover and what I saw next made the hair stand on the back of my neck. There was what looked like human hands. I was in total shock at this moment. The hands were thrown in like they were garbage. What kind of animal would do this?

I put the cover back on and stepped back. I gave myself a minute to compose myself. I asked myself: *What did I just find? What monster did this and who did these hands belong to? Was it the names of all the girls in the little book I found?* So much was going through my head. All I knew was, I needed to call Officer Burns and let him know what I had just uncovered.

I made my way toward the farmhouse and took a few more pictures. My hands were shaking, and my mind was racing. It was summer and the heat was blazing. No wonder the smell was sickening. I headed down the driveway to get to my car. As I got to my car, I leaned back and shook my head. I was in complete shock and just needed a minute to breathe. I opened my car and grabbed a bottle of water from my cooler. I had a few sips and jumped in my car. I sat for a few minutes until the air conditioning kicked in and cooled the car down.

I wasn't about to call Officer Burns. I thought it would be best to go see him at the station and show him what I came across today. I left and started to head down the dirt road until I got to the highway. As a few cars passed, it was safe to turn onto the highway. I put on some country music and tried to take my mind off what I had just discovered. I drove for about thirty minutes and finally got to town.

I went directly to the police station to see Officer Burns. I went inside and asked the secretary to let Officer Burns know I was there to see him." He is not here now," she told me. "He is out on an assignment and I'm not sure when he will be back. Is there anyone else you would like to see?" I told her, "No, I will get in touch with him another day, but thank you."

I left the station and went back to my car. I called Officer Burns from my cellphone. I was happy he answered his phone. He knew it was me and asked how I was doing. I told him where I went today and what I had found. I went into detail and said I took many pictures. "I'm almost done here; can you wait at the station for about half an hour? Or better yet, go grab a couple of coffee and I will meet you there. I will be leaving here soon and I'm not far away."

I told him I would go get coffee and see him soon. I left the station and went to get gas and grab a couple of coffees. I had a feeling this was going to be a long day. I got back to the station and headed inside with the coffee. I told the secretary Officer Burns was on his way back to meet me. She smiled and continued working on the computer.

I took a seat in the hallway and waited for him to get back to the station. After ten minutes, he walked through the door. He said, "Come with me to my office." We walked down the hall and went inside his office. I handed him his coffee and he said, "Thank you."

I explained how I'd found the old farmhouse and what I saw when I got there. "At first, I was just walking through it and looking around. I came across an old wooden box in a shed outside. It had a heavy chain wrapped around it, but I managed to get it off. I found some items like clothes and shoes. There was a couple of watches and purses. I kept looking and then I found a small book at the bottom. I opened it and flipped through the pages. There were names and dates written in the book. I found a bucket by a shed. I opened the bucket and find it full of human hands. I took a few pictures and that's when I made my way to my car."

I handed Officer Burns my phone so he could look through the pictures I took. He was in total shock at what he was looking at. "What in the world did you come across? What kind of sick animal would cut off hands and put them in a bucket? We need to get a crew there and look around. This can be, well, I'm not real sure what this can be. Is it OK for me to load these pictures onto my computer so we can have them? I need to call a team in and head over to the farmhouse. Can you write the directions down for me so we can get a team there? Did you happen to see a name or address on the farmhouse? It would be nice to be able to find out who owns the place and how long ago they lived there."

I hadn't noticed any name or numbers anywhere at the farmhouse. "I will write the directions down on a piece of paper while you go download the pictures off my phone. There was a locked gate at the end of the long driveway. I parked my car and walked up to the farmhouse. You might have to bring lock cutters to be able to drive all the way up the driveway."

Officer Burns went down the hall to download the pictures. He came back and said he had a team waiting to go to the farmhouse to look around. "I will be going with them to see what we are dealing with. I will be in touch as soon as I find out anything. Here is your phone back."

I left the station and headed home. It was still early, and the sun was out. I drove back to the cabin and waited for Officer Burns to call. I sat out on the deck for a couple of hours and still no call from Officer Burns. I hoped they'd found something that told them who these hands belonged to. I went inside at 7 p.m., to make some supper. It was still nice out, so I took my supper to the table outside. I sat and listened to the birds chirping. I could hear the traffic going up and down the highway.

It was getting late, so I went inside to watch TV. I guessed he wasn't going to call me tonight, so I went to bed. I knew it was going to be a restless night. I got up and opened the window to get a breeze to blow through. I stayed in bed and couldn't sleep. I tossed and turned. Finally, I got up and went outside to get some air. It was so hot in the cabin, even with the windows open.

The sky was bright with all the stars shining. I could hear the animals in the distance. It was so peaceful there; I could stay out on the deck all night. After about an hour, I went back inside to try to get some sleep. I left the windows open and went back to bed. I tossed and turned and looked at the clock every hour. At 6 a.m., I got out of bed and make a coffee. I went out on the deck, which I called "My Happy Place..

I sat outside listening to the birds until eight o'clock. I went in and made another coffee and grabbed my phone. I was hoping Officer Burns would call me soon. It was now after ten and he hadn't called yet. I couldn't wait any longer for him to call, so I went inside. I got dressed, grabbed a bottle of water, and went to my car. I was headed to the farmhouse to see if Officer Burns and his team were there. I wasn't about to have another sleepless night. I needed to know what had happened at that farmhouse.

I headed down the highway until I got to the turnoff for the farmhouse. I drove for about ten minutes, and I could see police cars parked up the long driveway. The gate was open, so I headed up the driveway, making my way to the front yard. I was stopped by an officer asking me what I was doing there. "I am here to see Officer Burns." He said, "I am Officer Gates; I will go find him for you."

I waited about ten minutes, then I could see Officer Burns heading toward me. He smiled as he got closer. "I'm sorry I didn't call you today, but it's been a real jackpot here. I have people working on trying to find out who owns this property. So far, we are hitting a dead end. My team has found several indications of bodies being buried on the property. They are digging up the pile of dirt that is in the pictures you showed me. The hands that were discovered, are all gone to be examined to determine who they belong to. We found another bucket of human hands, in the out-house. We are going to be here for several days, if not longer. We went through the book, and we have eighteen girls' names listed in it. We aren't sure if that has anything to do with the hands we found, but we are sure going to try to find out.

"I better get back to work and try to figure this out. These guys will be working around the clock until this gets resolved. We are going to set up lights and tarps to help with the digging. Anything we find will have to go out to be examined. I will call you tomorrow around lunchtime to give you an update."

I went to my car and headed down the driveway. There were police cars and people all over the farmhouse yard. I hoped they could figure this out and find out who owned the hands. I drove up and down a couple of roads before heading on the highway. There were a few cars driving around, looking at the police cars at the farmhouse. They are probably wondering what was going on there. I guessed it would be on the news in a few days or whenever they found something.

**I PUT MY WINDOWS** down and played some country music. The air was blowing through my car and I could smell the wildflowers as I drove down the highway. I loved to smell the flowers but never had luck growing them. I got back to my cabin and headed inside to make a sandwich. I made a chicken sandwich and took it outside to eat on the deck. I sat down and wanted to relax and enjoy the rest of my day.

I couldn't help but think about what they might find at the farmhouse. So much was going through my mind. What if someone killed these women and buried them there? There were so many names in that little book, and then the hands. Who would have done this and why? I went inside to make a phone call. I needed to take my mind off this and have a few laughs. I called my friend so we could catch up on things. It was always nice to keep in touch with close friends. We talked for over an hour about anything and everything.

I went for a walk down the road. I put my headset on and listened to my country music. It was such a beautiful day. I walked for about an hour and turned around and headed home. The air was fresh until you passed the farm animals. You could smell the horses and cows in the fields. I got back to the cabin after a very long walk. It was so nice to walk and clear my head. I wanted to enjoy my last few days before I started my courses.

I sat outside by the firepit and enjoyed the rest of the night. I roasted a couple of marshmallows over the fire. It had been a long time since I had one of those. They were sweet, so I couldn't eat too many. I sat outside for a couple of hours, then put water on the fire. I made sure it was out before I went inside.

After a piece of toast and a cup of tea, I watched TV, and went to bed. It was almost midnight, and it had been an adventurous day. I wanted to get up in the morning and spend time outside. I might take a drive back up around the farmhouse to see how things were going.

I woke at 3 a.m. to the sound of an ambulance going down the highway. I had my windows open and, because I am a light sleeper, it woke me up. I fell back asleep until 7 a.m. I felt well-rested and ready for the day. I never knew what I was doing until it happened. I enjoyed spending time outside and exploring around. I sat on the deck until about 10 a.m., and thought I'd better go inside and get ready to go. I wasn't sure where I was going, but knew it was for a drive.

I packed the cooler and grabbed a couple of water bottles, as I usually do. I liked to pack a light lunch just in case I was gone all day. I never knew where I would end up or what I would find. I left the cabin at 11:30 and headed down the highway. The traffic was flowing in a slow manner. I wasn't sure if they were just out for a weekend drive or just taking their time sightseeing. I wasn't in a hurry, so I just cruised and listened to my music. The drive was so relaxing, and the scenery was stunning. I could see the windmills in the distance and the mountains. There were so many colour-ful trees and the smell of wildflowers. I took in every breath and enjoyed it. I came across a dirt road and decided to drive down it. I didn't think I had ever been on this road before, so I thought I would go look around. I drove for about a half kilometre, then

I saw a black truck coming toward me. It looked like he was in a hurry. The rocks and dirt were flying in the air as he passed me. I could see that it was a male driver wearing a red baseball hat. He looked away from me as he passed by me. I thought: *Where is he going in such a hurry?*

I drove a little farther and came to a lookout area. I decided to take a break and stretch my legs. I grabbed my cellphone and took a few pictures. I could see the windmills and mountains from the lookout. I managed to get some nice pictures. I left and continued driving. I made it back on the highway and drove to the next nearest town. I could see a couple of signs showing a gas station. I figured there might be a store there.

I finally saw the garage station and a little store. I got out and started to head inside but I could see a closed sign on the door. I thought that was weird because it was the middle of the day and there were two cars in the parking lot. There was also a dark green van parked next to the door. I walked up to the van and looked inside. It didn't have anyone in it. I did see a few duffle bags in the back of the van. There were curtains over the windows in the back and sides.

I walked to the front of the store to look through the window. I was shocked to see two guys inside, holding a gun to a man's head. It looked like they were attempting to rob the store. I could also see a young girl, about seventeen. She looked so scared. I went to the side of the building and called the police. I told them where I was and what was going on inside.

The police told me to go to my car and lock the door. They were on their way. I didn't want to call Officer Burns. I knew he would be busy at the old farmhouse. I went around the back of the store to see if I could find a door. I thought maybe I could sneak inside and listen to what was going on. There was a door at the back of the store, but it was locked. I looked in the window but couldn't see anything or anyone. I could hear yelling coming from inside. It seemed like forever for the police to get there. I was waiting and waiting and finally I could hear a girl yelling. "Let me go, let me go." I ran quietly to the front of the store. I was on the side up against the building. I didn't want to get caught. I could see two guys with masks on, put the girl in their van. They had guns, so I wasn't about to intervene. I took a few pictures and got the license plate.

The van pulled away and I went inside. I wanted to make sure the guy inside was not hurt. I couldn't see him at first, but as I walked around the counter, there he was, lying on the floor in a pool of blood. I checked for a pulse, but there was none. He was gone. I didn't hear a gunshot, so it must have been a stabbing. I called the police back and they were almost there. After a couple of minutes, the police arrived.

They came inside to find me with the guy behind the counter. "Over here, over here. I am the one who called the police. Please help him. I don't think he is alive. I can't find a pulse and there is blood everywhere." They checked him and said he was dead. They introduced themselves and asked me what happened. I gave them the description of the van and informed them they had taken a young girl with them. They called for backup and for the coroner and detectives to come to the store.

"How many men were here, and can you give me a description? Anything you can remember can be helpful. The littlest detail can be very important."

"There were two men wearing masks. They were both about five foot ten with medium builds. One guy was wearing a grey hoody with a black baseball cap. He had on blue jeans and white runners. The other guy was wearing a black hoody, jeans, and black runners. One guy had a gun on the girl and the other guy was carrying a knife. They told the girl to get in the back of the van. The guy with the knife got in the back of the van with her; the other guy wearing the black cap got in the driver's side. They drove away and that's when I went inside."

"I will need the description of the van and the plate number, please. It looks like there are two cars here, so we can run them through to see if we can get an ID on the girl and the guy behind the counter. I am going to put an alert out on the van. We need to find them before they hurt the girl. I am going inside to see if they have any surveillance cameras in there that may help us identify the two guys. I have your statement and your name. If we need anything else, we will contact you. Thank you for all your help and being here at the right time."

I left the store and headed down the highway in the direction the van had gone. It was possible that I might come across the van and be able to help the girl they took. There was a steady flow of traffic on the highway. It was such a nice day; I was sure people were out for a drive. I passed a few lookoffs but didn't see any sign of the green van.

I drove for at least another hour and decided I should head back the other way. I was going in the opposite direction of where I lived. I turned around and headed toward home. I was at least two hours away from town at this point. There was a lot of traffic, and I was just taking my time in case I saw the van. It could have turned around and gone in the other direction. I finally got to town and saw no signs of the van. I hoped the police could find the girl before something happened to her.

I went to the grocery store on my way through town before I headed back home to the cabin. It was still early enough to enjoy the rest of the day on the deck. I might even get some outside work done around the yard. I picked up a few things I needed and headed home. I wasn't in any mood to make supper, so I picked up a sub and brought it home to eat. I sat on the deck with my sub and ate while listening to the birds. It was so peaceful and relaxing. I went inside to get my speaker so I could put on some old country music. It reminded me of my dad when I played my country music.

After about an hour on the deck, my phone rang. It was Officer Burns. "I have some news about the farmhouse. We have found a total of nine women buried in the pile of dirt that was covered with the shrubs and grass. We are still looking on the property for more bodies. The hands came back as being a total of twenty-eight. All left hands of the victims were cut off. We have not identified anyone yet. Everything we find will have to be sent out to be analyzed and hopefully we can ID the bodies. The bodies and the hands were decomposed and have been there for many years. This may take a long time to solve. I have a team going through missing persons dating back twenty years or more. We are still trying to find out the owner of the property. This may help us solve this case.

"We have officers going to some of the locals that live in the surrounding area, to see if they have any information on anyone who may have lived here in the past. It's a long shot, but we need answers to be able to help with the investigation.

"I am shocked but relieved at the same time. I knew it felt creepy there. This may bring closure to some of the victims' families if we can ID these people."

Officer Burns continued to tell me that he would be at the farmhouse for at least the rest of the week or until they wrapped things up. "I have every available person on this case. There is so much ground to cover and so many places to look. We must make sure to cover every inch of this place. We found nine bodies and we are sure there are more here somewhere. I have my men working around the clock on this case. I will be in touch in a few days to update you on our findings. Good luck with your courses next week."

I said, "Thank you and keep in touch." I sat back and sighed. What a discovery I had found. How many bodies were buried there at the old farmhouse? So many questions I wanted answered.

I wished I was there to help, but I guessed I helped by finding the farmhouse.

I went inside and made a coffee. I turned the news on and sat to relax. As I was watching the news, I heard them say, "There was a robbery today at a gas station. One man was killed, and a girl was taken hostage. Later today, the van was recovered in a wooded area, and the girl was found unharmed. Two men were taken into custody. Thank you to a good Samaritan for being in the right place at the right time. We had a witness who came forward and help solve this case and save a girl's life today."

Wow, that sure made me feel good that they found the girl. I had been worried about her and what they might have done to her. I was glad she was found unharmed. I spent the rest of the evening talking to a few friends on the phone. It was time to catch up on our own news.

I went to bed early and had a good sleep. At 7 a.m., I went outside to have my coffee. The cabin was stuffy and so hot. There was a nice breeze out, so I sat on the deck and enjoyed it.

At about 9 a.m., my phone rang, and it was the officer who was on scene from the gas station. He said, "I don't know if you heard yet, but the girl and the two suspects were located. The girl was found safe and unharmed. The two guys were arrested but we would like you to come down and ID them, if you could. They will be in custody until their court date, but we need your statement. As of now, they are both denying having anything to do with the killing of the guy at the gas station. The girl they abducted is also a witness to the stabbing. She saw the one guy slice his throat and leave him for dead. Are you able to come to the station at noon today?"

"I most definitely will be there today at noon. See you then and thank you."

**I GOT READY AND** headed to town. The highway was busy with traffic, so I took my time driving in while listening to music. I put the windows down and cruised in until I got to the station. The parking lot was empty, other than police cars. I went inside and checked in at the front desk. A few minutes later, I was taken to a room. After I gave my statement and made the ID on the two men, I left. It didn't take me long. I was in and out in thirty minutes.

I was in town and didn't feel like going back home, so I went for a drive. I headed in the opposite direction, where I knew there were some old, vacant houses. I stopped at a store and got a bottle of water and a bag of chips. It wasn't much, but it was something to hold me over. I drove until I got to a turn with a big sign. The sign was cut in half and covered in red spray paint. I couldn't make out anything on the sign. I turned down the road and kept driving. I'd heard people talk about houses down that road and I never got to check it out. Well, I guess today was the day to explore. I passed a few vehicles along the way. I kept driving until the road branched off to another one. I turned down the road and drove farther.

After about ten minutes, I noticed a girl by herself, walking up the road toward me. She looked tired and was wearing one shoe.

She was waving her arms for me to stop. I pulled over to the side and stopped my car.

As I got out, she screamed, "Please help me. I have been beaten and left for dead by my husband. I have been here all night down over the bank." I asked her what her name was, and she said it was Rosa. "Please help me. I don't want him to come back."

I said, "You are safe now. Let's get you to a hospital."

She continued, "But you don't understand—he has my son. He is running away with my son and said I would never see him again. He beat me and threw me over the bank. I must have been knocked out for a while. When I woke up, I tried climbing back up to the top. It took me hours to make it back up. I kept falling and trying to climb over the rocks.

"I don't want to go to the hospital, please take me to the police so they can find my son."

I said, "I will take you, but you need a doctor to check you over. I will call the police to meet us at the hospital." Rosa agreed to go to the hospital if the police would meet us there.

I called the police and gave them all the information. I told them I had Rosa with me, and that we were heading to the hospital. "Her husband has their six-year-old son and he said he was leaving with him. He told Rosa she would never see him again." The officer said he would meet us there to get all the information.

I got Rosa in the car, and we turned around on the dirt road. We headed in the direction of the highway. I needed to get her to the hospital, and we needed to find her son. She was so scared. "Please drive faster. I need to find my son. If he leaves the country, I may never get him back."

I drove as fast and safe as I could to get on the highway. There was traffic both ways, so I waited to be able to pull out safely. We were about a twenty-five-minute drive from town. I talked to Rosa to keep her calm. She was crying and wanted her son back. "He is only six years old, and he needs his mommy. My husband had an affair, so I told him I wanted a divorce and he snapped. He said he would never give me a divorce and I would never keep our son from him."

We finally got to the hospital and went inside. Rosa saw the police car and she ran to the door. The parking lot was full of cars. We went to the front desk to check in, but the officer intervened. "I am Officer Hill, please come with me," he said. "You must be Rosa."

We went down the long, narrow hall until we got to a private room. Two officers and a nurse came in the room with us. I told the officer, "I am the one who found Rosa." He asked me to wait outside, but Rosa wanted me to stay with her. "Please let her stay with me. She saved my life and I feel safe with her being here." Officer Hill was fine with my staying.

As Officer Hill was asking Rosa questions, the nurse was trying to examine her cuts and bruises. The nurse asked Rosa where she was hurting and if she had any broken bones. Rosa said, "Just leave me alone. I just want to find my son. Please find my son," she pleaded with the officer.

As Rosa spoke to the officer, there were tears running down her tired-looking face. "My husband is driving a red Chev pickup truck. His name is Joe Gillis, and he is thirty-eight years old. He is six feet tall and weighs about 210 pounds. He has blue eyes and short blonde hair. My son is Nickolas, but we call him Nick, and he is six years old. He is forty-five pounds and has short blonde hair. Please find my son."

Officer Hill said he was going to go put out a search for the truck and do everything to find her son. "We have all the information we need, so I will leave you get your injuries looked after. I will be back in thirty minutes to talk again."

I stayed with Rosa as the nurse asked her several questions about her injuries. "I see blood on your head, so I need to look. Your legs are cut, and you have blood on the side of your face.

Do you have any broken bones or any places that may require an X-ray?"

Rosa said, "No, just what you see. Please clean me up so I can leave. I can't just sit here. I must go look for my son."

The nurse cleaned up all the blood and closed a few open wounds. Rosa was on edge and just wanted to leave. I sat with her and held her hand. We will be done soon, and we can leave. After about forty-five minutes, Officer Hill came back. We have all the information, and we are looking for his truck. Is there any idea where he would take your son? Do you have a summer home or cabin? Is here a favourite place they might go? Any information may be helpful to be able to find them.

Rosa said, "No. I have no idea other than my son loves to play baseball at his favourite park. The park is a five-minute walk from our house."

"OK, we will check out the area. We will have an officer take you home and stay parked outside your home just in case he shows up."

Rosa thanked me for saving her life and helping her. "If it wasn't for you, I may have never been rescued. I am so grateful you found me down that dirt road. I will always remember what you did." I gave Rosa my phone number and told her to call me anytime. She gave me a hug and left with the officer.

I left the hospital and headed home. I drove through town first and got a few groceries. I wanted to get back home and sit outside. My courses were starting tomorrow, so I needed to get things ready. I was excited and scared at the same time.

**I BROUGHT IN MY** three bags of groceries and put everything away. I made a sandwich and went out on the deck. It was sunny and it had been an eventful day. I couldn't help but think about Rosa and if they would find her son. She must be so scared and hurt at what her husband did.

I went inside at 7 p.m., and got a few things ready for tomorrow. It would take me about twenty-five minutes to get to town and find a parking spot. My course was from eight to three, Monday to Friday. My night class was on Wednesday from six to nine. I went to bed at 11 p.m.

It was a beautiful sunny morning and time to get ready to go to my course. I sat outside for a few minutes, drinking my coffee. I packed a lunch and got my things ready to head to town. I left my cabin at 7:15, so I could find the place and get settled in the class.

I found the building and went inside. I stopped at the desk to ask where Room 212 was. "Just take the elevator to the left and go to the second floor. The rooms all have numbers on the doors. You shouldn't have a problem finding it."

I said, "Thank you," and headed to the elevator.

I found the classroom and went inside. The window was open and there were two ladies sitting down. I sat down and got settled.

After a few minutes, a few more people arrived and took a seat. At 7:50, a young gentleman entered the class and said, "Good morning, I am your instructor. My name is Ken. We should have eight students, so we will get started in a few minutes.

"I have a paper for all of you to read over before we get started. Please come up and get one and read and sign it. You will also be given a textbook that will have to be returned after this course, so please take care of it."

At 8:05, our class started. We ended up with seven students instead of eight. Ken went to the front of the class and started writing on the board. I knew this was going to be a long few months.

After class, I left and headed home. The more notes I took, the better I could study. I got home and made supper. The birds were chirping, and the sun was out. It was another beautiful day.

My phone rang and it was Officer Burns. He said, "I just wanted to let you know that we have found twenty-seven bodies at the farmhouse. We searched every inch of the property, inside and out. We are still working on who lived there and where they are now. These bodies are believed to have been here for twenty years or more. There will have to be more investigating to try to piece this all together. We are sending everything to be analyzed. We also found several bodies in the outhouse buried under the floor. We are confident there are no more bodies on the property. This has been a long few weeks, but worth every minute. We need to bring closure to the families as soon as we can ID them."

I was relieved it was over. I told Officer Burns I had started my course and would start my night course this week. I was looking forward to the self-defence course. He wished me luck and said goodbye.

I sat outside for over an hour. It was so peaceful and relaxing. I could hear the traffic going up and down the highway. I went inside and did my dishes. I sat down and went over the work we did today. I knew there was so much to learn, and I needed to study every night. I really wanted to work with the police and needed a high mark to do so.

I was heading back into the school to get this course done. The drive in was slow today. I was behind a truck that was taking his time. After my class, I headed home. On my drive home, my phone rang, but I didn't answer it. I wanted to wait until I get home and I would check my messages.

I went inside to make a coffee and came out to sit on the deck. It was so hot and the chairs on the deck were too hot to sit on. I went inside to get a towel to lay on the chair. I put my music on low and sat and relaxed.

I checked my messages and the call I had missed was from Rosa. She asked me to call her back. I dialed the number and she answered. She said, "I have my son back and I owe it all to you. The police found him with his father in a hotel. He is safe, thanks to you. I owe you my life for saving my son. I don't know how I will ever thank you enough. I am happy and relieved he is found." I told Rosa I was happy to help and glad she got her son Nick back.

Well, that sure was a happy day for everyone. Now to go inside and watch the news. I sat with my feet up and the window open. There was a nice breeze blowing through. As I watched the news, there was a broadcast that came up about a kidnapped baby at the local hospital. It said a two-day-old baby girl was taken from her bassinet in her mom's room. They were looking for a lady in her thirties with a small build and red hair. She was wearing a light blue uniform with white runners. The outside surveillance showed them getting in a white pickup truck. If you had any leads, you were to please contact your local police department.

The news made me think about everything going on in the world right then. It was so unfair not to feel safe anymore. I hoped they found this baby girl soon and got her home safe to her mom.

I pulled out my books and went over my work from that day's class. This was going to be a long course but well worth it when I was done. I enjoyed working with the police and helping people.

I had a good night sleep and headed into class. This week was finally over, and I got to enjoy the weekend. I was planning an adventure but not sure where I would be going. I usually decided after I got up and had a coffee. I stopped by the grocery store after my class was done. The traffic was heavy, and the stores were busy. I grabbed the few things I needed and headed home to the cabin. I was glad to get home and sit on the deck. I ate supper and put a fire on in the fire pit. It was peaceful and relaxing to just sit and breathe. I roasted a few marshmallows and sat for hours, enjoying my time alone.

It was Saturday morning and, after a good night's sleep, I got up and made a coffee. I sat outside thinking about where to go that day. I went in to get ready and packed the cooler. I was leaving for the day. I grabbed a couple bottles of cold water and put them on ice. I headed out on the highway at about 10 a.m.

The traffic was going slower than usual, but I just went with it. I was listening to my country music and had the windows down. The breeze was blowing through, and it felt good. I drove until I saw a look off. There were a few cars there, so I pulled in to get a look. I wanted to take pictures of the scenery. I heard a man yell to someone down below. "Are you OK?" Do you need help? "The man saw someone down over the bank. As I looked over to see what he was looking at, I saw a girl lying on the ground. She looked like she had fallen over the bank. I was looking around to try to find a place to climb down to help her. The man said he was going down to help and for me to stay up and call for help. I told him to be careful and not to slip. He said he would go slow and stay with her until help arrived. I ran to my car and gave him a bottle of water to take to her.

I called for help and the man headed down to the girl. It was a nice day and there was lots of traffic. I was not sure how she ended up so far down. I didn't see any vehicle down there that might have gone over. I was a little confused at how she got there. I could see the man taking his time but sliding down, for the most part. I didn't want to see him fall and get hurt. He finally arrived safely to where the girl was. I could see him trying to help her and sit her up. She was covered in blood from what I could see. It didn't look like she was responding to him. She looked limp and not moving. He hollered, "We need help right away—she is not responding. She is covered in blood and hurt bad."

I yelled back, "Help is on the way."

After a few minutes, I saw a man come out from behind a tree and approach the man with the lady. I could see a struggle and then I heard a gunshot. The man shot the guy who was trying to help the lady on the ground. I was trying to figure out what just happened. Was this the man who tried to hurt the lady? The man with the gun ran off into the woods. I told a few people that help was on the way, and they now needed to call the police. I was going down the bank to try to help these people. "Tell the police, the man who fired a shot, is running through the woods. The man is wearing jeans and a black baseball cap. He has on a black T-shirt and white runners. Give this description to the police when they arrive."

I went down the side of the bank and took my time climbing down. I slid most of the way, but needed to get there to help. I arrived on scene and the guy had been shot once in the abdomen. I put pressure on it and told him help was on the way. I couldn't find a pulse on the girl. She was covered in blood and lying lifeless on the ground. I looked at her and found a gunshot to the back of her neck. She was not breathing or moving. I knew she was dead, so I went to help the man. I needed to keep him awake and talk to him. I asked him his name and he said it was Jason. I asked him a few questions and made sure he stayed awake. He talked about his wife and little girl and how much they meant to him. I said, "Help is on the way, and you need to stay awake." He asked me if the girl was alive, and I said no. I could see a tear roll down his face. "All I wanted to do was help her. Why did someone shoot me? Who was that guy with the gun?"

"I have no idea, but we will get to the bottom of it."

I could hear the ambulance from up above. They were trying to get down the bank to evaluate the situation. I yelled, "We have a man shot, please hurry!" As the paramedics made their way down the bank, I could hear the police cars approaching. They arrived and made their way down the bank to find the girl deceased, and the man needing to go to the hospital. "They are going to take good care of you and get you to a hospital." They made their way up with the man on the stretcher, covered in blood.

I climbed back up the bank, where more police had arrived on scene. I gave a statement and my phone number to call if they needed more information. I told them the girl down the bank had been shot and left for dead. They thanked me and headed down the bank to where the girl was.

I left and went on my drive a little farther down the highway. I listened to the radio, had the windows down, and the wind blowing through. What a day this had turned out to be. I drove for about another hour, then turned around and went in the other direction. Why would someone just kill someone in cold blood and shoot another person?

I drove until I reached the highway to get back home to the cabin. I was about an hour from the cabin, so I took my time. There was so much traffic on the highway, it made the drive home slower than usual. As I reached my driveway, I noticed a moose in my yard. I slowly made my way up my driveway to try to get some pictures. I got out and managed to snap a few pictures before the moose decided to go deep into the woods. This is what living in a cabin in the woods feels like. The peacefulness and watching the animals.

I went inside and grabbed a cold drink. I sat out on the deck for a couple of hours. I thought about my day. A girl found deceased and an innocent guy trying to help. I hope the guy pulled through and they found who did this.

I went inside to get my chicken to put on the barbecue. I turned on the news while I peeled potatoes. I heard them say they'd found the missing baby who was taken from the hospital. I was so relieved she had been found safe and unharmed. "A lady in her thirties was arrested today in the kidnapping of a two-day-old baby from a local hospital. The lady was seen today in a park, sitting on a bench, holding the baby. A witness said, "She was just sitting there, singing a lullaby to the baby. I knew it was her because of the description the news had given. I sat beside the lady, and she just kept singing the same song over and over. 'You are safe now and nobody will hurt you.' That's when I knew it was the baby from the hospital. I left the bench and called the police. I watched from a distance until the police arrived."

**I COOKED SUPPER OUTSIDE** as I relaxed. It was such a nice sunny day and too hot to cook inside. I had to enjoy every weekend I could. I was not used to being back in school five days a week. I had my night course to go to, as well.

It was a busy week and lots of studying every night. My course was going well, and so was the self- defence one. I enjoy getting out with other people and learning how to defend myself. It is important in this line of work to be able to protect yourself. I hope I am not put in a situation that I need to protect myself from violence.

I got a call from Officer Burns as I was enjoying my coffee on the deck. He said they were preparing for a huge undercover case and they would need me to work with them. "How are the courses going?"

I said, "They are going good. I am studying every night and learning so much. The self-defence course is also going well." I laughed and said, "I will be able to kick butt soon."

He chucked and said, "We need you soon, so keep up the good work. We have a case that needs to be shut down. It's a drug and prostitution ring that's happening in our own town. These girls are taken off the streets and given a place to live and being taken care of. They are then forced into prostitution and drugs. We believe there are at least three homes and roughly twenty girls working with this group." I told him I would be glad to help when I was done my courses.

Day after day, week after week, I went to school. I felt like I had learnt so much and this would help me when I was out in the field. I needed to learn safety and how things were done by the book.

It was Friday, and I had a test in the morning. I'd studied all week for hours and I was ready for this. I went to class and Ken handed me my test. "You have all day to finish this, so please take your time," Ken said. "You will need to get an 85 percent on this test, or you will be required to rewrite it. You can only rewrite the test once. If you fail the test the second time, you will not be able to finish this course. You can re-apply in a year. Good luck, everyone."

The classroom was very quiet while people went over their tests. The sun was shining through the windows, and you could hear people walking in the hallway. I couldn't wait for this day to be over. I wanted to take my time and make sure not to rush through it. I needed to pass, I wanted to pass. I was eager to work in the field.

I sat and looked the test over and then began to write. I had some multiple-choice and some written questions to answer. It was going well, and I didn't seem to be struggling. It was very quiet in the class. The instructor, Ken, was sitting at his desk, reading a book. He said, "If anyone needs a break, feel free to go, one at a time." A girl got up and left the room. She seemed like she was frustrated as she got up to leave. The rest of us kept working on our tests. I just wanted to concentrate and get it done. At about 11:00, I finished the test and looked it over. I got up from my desk and handed it to Ken. He said, "If you are done, you can leave, and I will see you Monday." I left and went to my car. I felt like I did well on the test but had to wait until Monday to get my mark.

I headed to the grocery store to pick up a few things I needed. It was the weekend, and I needed an adventure. I'd studied hard all week and deserved a break from everything. I'd heard about a private camping place, not too far from there. I wanted to see if I could find it. It was apparently in the woods, where nobody would bother you. There was a waterfall there and a beach. That was my plan today: Go try to find this place. I had a good idea where it was.

After finally getting home, it was that time of day to make a cold drink and sit outside on the deck. The sun was shining, and the hummingbirds were drinking from my feeders. I wanted to get as much sun as I could before it went behind the clouds. I was planning a trip tomorrow in the woods to find this camping site people had been talking about. I sat outside until it got a little darker. I decided to put a fire on in the fire pit and sit around it. I gathered some wood and started a fire. I went inside to make a chicken sandwich to take outside with me. I pulled up a lawn chair and had a seat by the pit. It was such a beautiful evening; I didn't want to go inside anytime soon. I could hear the animals howl. It sounded like a wolf or coyote in the distance. I could hear the traffic on the highway and see the headlights through the trees.

I stayed outside enjoying this beautiful evening. I knew I had to go inside soon so I could get some sleep. It was going to be a long day tomorrow and lots of walking. I put water on the fire and made sure it was out before I slowly made my way inside for the night.

I cut up some veggies and made a sandwich to take with me. I packed some fruit and granola bars. I wanted to head out around 9 a.m. to try to find this place. I went to bed at 11 p.m. I left the window open to try to get a breeze blowing through.

**I WOKE AT 6** a.m., to the sound of birds chirping. I knew it was time to get up and have a coffee on the deck. It was a beautiful, sunny morning, and I had a day planned. I was excited about going on an adventure today in the woods.

I went inside to get ready and head on my adventure. I got dressed and packed the cooler and my backpack. I made sure my phone was fully charged and that I had a few bottles of cold water. I grabbed my walking shoes as I left the cabin to head to my car.

I opened my car windows and cranked the music so loud, I think the trees shook. I was rolling down the highway like I didn't have a care in the world. This was what made me happy and relaxed. I drove for about an hour until I reached the road to turn onto. There wasn't a sign, but there was a large barrel on the left side of the entrance. That's what people said to look for. The barrel had a bright blue painted cover and a happy face painted in yellow, on the front. I knew it had to be the right place and, if not, I would turn around.

I drove for about ten minutes and came across two cars parked. Nobody was around, so I decided to park and walk through the woods. I grabbed my backpack and put a bottle of water in it. I changed into my runners and grabbed my phone. I put a baseball cap on and locked my car. I could see a trail where it looked like people used. I was sure this was the way to the camp site and the beach. I thought I would give it a try and see where it took me.

I didn't see anyone as I walked through the trail. The trail was steep and very rocky. I slipped a few times, but managed to keep my balance. I kept going until I came to an open area. There were about four different paths to take. Now it became a guessing game on which one to take. I didn't want to get lost, but I wanted to see where I would end up. I just randomly started heading down the trail to the right. I'm not sure why I chose that one, but I did.

I walked on a trail that kept leading into different directions. I wasn't sure where I was going at this point. I was trying to remember which trail I'd taken so I could make it back out safely. I kept walking, and it seemed like hours had passed. I hadn't seen a single soul on any of the trails. I couldn't hear anything except the birds chirping and twigs cracking under my feet. I felt like I was walking in circles. I knew now I was probably going to have a hard time finding my way out of there.

I could hear what sounded like a flock of birds just up ahead. I walked in that direction until I came to a sudden halt. I saw a few trees ahead of me, but what I saw next was disturbing. There was a human wrapped around a tree with rope. I went to get a closer look and could tell it was a young male who was tied to the tree. He was half-dressed and covered in blood. He was beaten so badly, I wouldn't recognize him if I knew him. I was shocked to have come across this in the middle of nowhere. The guy had no shirt on and was cut and marked like he had been tortured. The blood was pooled to the ground, and he looked like he had been there for days. I needed to get help, but I didn't even know where I was.

I tried my cellphone but had no service. I decided I had to try to find my way back to my car so I could call for help. I went back on the same trail, but after about twenty-five minutes, things were getting confusing as I didn't know which way to go. There were so many different trails to take. I sat for a minute and had a drink of water. I felt confused but had to try to get back to my car. It was hot and I was tired of going in circles. Hours had passed and I wasn't anywhere near getting back to my car.

I had to try my best to get out of the woods before it got dark. I tried my phone, but I still didn't have service. The twigs were snapping as I walked, and the birds were flying above me. I had no idea where I was. It was hot and I was tired. My feet were burning from all the walking. I couldn't give up, so I kept going and going, hoping something along the way would look familiar.

I walked, which felt like miles and miles. I still had no idea where I was or how to get back to my car. I was running out of water, and it was hot. I sat on a rock and ate a sandwich and had some fruit. I needed to eat to keep my energy. I could see down the trail and there was nothing but trees and brush. I had no idea if I was going the right way or not.

I started down the trail and tripped on a tree stump. I rolled and rolled until I got to the bottom. I was roughed up and bleeding from the knee. My leg was hurt, and my hands were full of cuts. I didn't have anything to stop the bleeding in my knee. I used a leaf and cleaned it up as best I could. I knew I was in trouble and needed to get out of there before dark. I had no way of contacting anyone and my phone was going to die. I decided to shut my phone off for a while and try again later.

My legs were cut and bleeding and my hands were sore. I had rocks in my hands under the skin. I was a complete mess, but had to keep going. I wasn't about to give up. I continued walking and walking for hours. It was going to be dark soon and I had no idea where I was or how far I was from my car. I didn't have a sweater or a lighter to start a fire to stay warm. I was walking in circles, so I decided I should gather up some brush and try to make a little shelter. It was getting dark, and I knew I wasn't about to find my way out of there now.

I walked around to try to find a couple of large trees to make a shelter out of. I gathered some brush and made a comfy place to sit and try to stay warm. I knew I wasn't going to get any sleep, but I had to stay warm and safe until daylight. I tried my phone but still had no cell service, so I shut it off to save power. I had a little bit of food to eat until tomorrow. I was almost out of water. I sat listening to the animals for hours. I was getting cold and thirsty. My water was all gone, and my body was shivering. It wasn't too cold, but I was sore from the fall and hurt all over. I just had to make it through the night and wait for daylight to find my way out of there.

I curled up in a ball and must have fallen asleep. I woke up and was still shivering. I could hear the animals in the distance. I wasn't sure what time it was, but just wanted to see the sunrise so I could start walking and find my way out. I was not prepared for this. I had never spent the night lost in the woods. It was not a good feeling, but you needed to be strong to survive. I stood up and stretched my body and walked back and forth to keep warm.

Finally, I could see the sunrise. I knew it was going to be light soon and I could finally try to find my way out. I just had to have patience and wait. My legs were sore, and my body felt like I had been hit by a truck. I gathered up my stuff and started to walk again. I walked up and down trails for hours and hours. I didn't feel like I was getting anywhere except lost and farther into the woods. What was I going to do? How was I going to find my way out of there?

I continued walking until I found a trail that looked like it had traffic from people using it. I could see a bit of garbage on the sides of the trail. I had to take this one just in case it took me the right way. I walked and walked, getting hurt by the twigs, stumbling over the rocks, and being cut by the bushes. I wasn't sure if I was going the right way, but had to keep moving. I got to the top and saw two dirt roads going in different directions. I took the one to the left and kept walking.

I walked about thirty minutes and came to a dead end. I am so tired at this point. I sat and rested for a few minutes. I turned on my cell phone but still had no service. I walked back the way I came and decided to take the other dirt road and see where that one went.

I made my way down the other dirt road, and it was going for miles. I didn't see anyone and continued walking. It was hot and the bugs were out. I was so tired and sore. I was thirsty and hungry. I walked and walked until finally I thought I heard people talking. I stopped and leaned against a tree. I waited and then I could see two people walking toward me.

I yelled, "Help!"

They came running and asked if I was hurt. "What happened to you?" the young girl asked.

I told them I had gotten lost and spent the night in the woods. I needed to find my way to my car. "The cars are parked about a mile up the trail in the parking lot," said the girl. "Let us help you back to your car."

I said, "No, it's OK if I know that I am close to the parking lot. I can make it from here, but thank you so much for your help. I wouldn't want to spend another night out here alone."

I slowly headed up the trail to reach my car. Finally, I could see the parking lot. My car was right where I'd left it. I was never so happy to be out of the woods. My happy place had just become my not-so-happy place. I never did find the campsite I was looking for.

I opened my car and grabbed a bottle of water. It wasn't cold, but it was wet and it sure felt good guzzling it down. I ate some soggy fruit and sat and put the air conditioning on. I turned my phone on and headed back home. I needed to call the police to let them know about the guy tied to the tree. I wasn't sure if I could ever find that place again. I had walked around lost for so many hours. I wasn't sure how the police would ever find the guy who was tied to the tree.

I shut the air off and opened the windows. I needed a breeze blowing through. I needed a shower and to get my cuts cleaned up. I got through the heavy traffic on the highway. I swear, when you are in a hurry, the traffic feels so much slower. I took my time—or at least I thought I did. I was tired and just wanted to get cleaned up and to rest. I got home to the cabin and went inside, carrying my cooler and backpack. I made it up the steps and unlocked the door. It felt good to be back home and not to have to spend another night in the woods. I was glad to have come across a couple of people to be able to tell me where the parking lot was. I had never been so happy to see my car.

**I QUICKLY JUMPED IN** the shower to get cleaned up. I washed the blood off my body and watched it go down the drain. I was sore and had so many scratches and bruises. I got out and put ice on my knee. I covered up a few cuts with bandages so they wouldn't look so bad. It felt so good to just let the shower run over my sore, achy body.

After I got out and got into something comfortable, I called Officer Burns. I wanted to let him know what I had found and hopefully get someone in the area to look for the man. I sat outside on the deck and called him. I filled him in on my adventure in the woods.

"We need to get a group of people together and try to find the man," said Officer Burns. "Is there any way you could try to remember some points of interest or something that would help us find him? We need to try to find this guy."

"I remember going in so many directions and then I came across the guy tied to the tree. I left to go get help, and that's when I was walking in circles. I got lost and it was getting dark. I made a spot to stay warm for the night using branches and leaves. I bundled myself up in a ball to stay warm. I was hurt and scared.

I fell and hurt my knee. I am full of cuts and bruises, but I knew I had to survive.

I gave him the best directions I could and the area I was in. He thanked me and said he would be sending a crew to try to find the guy. They would have a few hours before it got dark. I would be in touch as soon as I knew more. "Get some rest and feel better," said Officer Burns.

We hung up the phone and I put my phone on charge. I put everything away that I had with me. I made a salad and a cup of tea. It felt good to sit and relax in my La-Z-Boy chair. I turned the TV on and must have fallen asleep. I woke at 8 p.m. I was sore when I woke up and felt stiff. My knee was throbbing, and my legs hurt. I knew there was nothing broken. It was just going to take time to heal. Well, I guessed I wouldn't be going on an adventure tomorrow. I would stay home and try and heal and rest my knee. I hoped they had luck finding the guy I'd seen tied to the tree.

I went out on the deck for an hour before I went to bed. I enjoyed listening to the animals in the distance and looking at the stars. The sky was so bright tonight. It was peaceful and relaxing. It was good to be home and to be able to sleep in my own bed.

I went inside and climbed into bed. I tossed and turned for a couple of hours. My knee was throbbing, so I got up and sat in my La-Z-Boy chair. I had to elevate my leg and it felt so much better. I fell asleep with the window open and a soft breeze blowing through the cabin. The fresh air felt so good and smelt like wildflowers.

I woke at 6 a.m. to shooting pains through my legs. I must have gotten stiff sitting in a chair all night. I couldn't bend my knee. I got some ice and put it on the sore area. I sat in my chair for an hour with the ice on my knee. I had to get up and move around. I couldn't just sit and do nothing.

I spent the day lounging and walking around the yard. The sun was hot and there was no breeze. I had to go to school tomorrow and hopefully get a high mark on the test I wrote on Friday.

I went for a walk on the road but was too sore to continue. I came back home after about ten minutes. I knew I was pushing myself but that's just who I am. I soaked in the tub for a half hour and relaxed. After I got out, I watched TV, and went to bed at 11:00. I felt like every bone in my body was aching. I managed to get a couple hours of sleep and finally had to get out of bed at 6 a.m. I'd had enough of lying there in pain. I needed to move around. I sat on the deck with my coffee. I could hear the traffic going down the highway, the planes flying above, and the animals in the distance.

I went inside to get ready for my course. I packed a lunch and headed in. I got to class and took a seat. After everyone was in class, Ken walked around and handed us our tests we'd written on Friday. I looked at mine and I had a 96 percent. I was so happy I'd passed and with such a high mark. After class, we all got up to leave. "Are you all right?" said Ken. "I couldn't help but notice the pain you are in."

"I will be fine," I said. "I was out exploring and fell down a bank. I got lost in the woods and had to spend the night, but managed to get back to my car the next day. I was lucky. I wouldn't want to do that again."

"I am glad you are OK," said Ken. "Go home and get some rest and I will see you tomorrow."

I left and walked down the hall to find the instructor who taught my night course. I needed to tell him I would be there, but may not be able to participate right away. I found him and explained what had happened. "Just show up and you can learn by watching, and I hope you feel better soon," he said.

I left and went to my car to head home to call Officer Burns. I was curious if they'd found the guy that was tied to the tree. I hoped they were able to figure out where he was.

I went through town on this sunny afternoon with a steady flow of traffic. I had to get gas in my car, and I grabbed a coffee in the drive-through. I headed home, but the traffic was slow. I was behind a school bus that stopped to let students off. I played country music and had my windows open for the fresh air. I love driving but not today with a sore knee. I couldn't wait to get home to relax and put my feet up.

As I got back to the cabin, my phone rang. It was Officer Burns. "We didn't have any luck finding the man tied to the tree. My men are still there looking and have been all over the area since yesterday. They are mapping it all out, but still no sign of the man. Can you remember anything that would help locate him?"

"I think I told you everything I know about where I went. After I got lost, I was going in circles and couldn't find my way anywhere. It was getting dark, so I had to stop and take cover for the night. I had a hard time finding my way out, and if it wasn't for the people I met, I might still be there. They showed me which way to go to get back to my car. I don't remember much because I was hurt, cold, and sore. I was tired and hungry, and my knee was throbbing. I hope they find him and give his family closure; they need to find out who did this."

Officer Burns said the search would continue until the next day and, after that, they would have covered most of the area. "We are hopeful he will be found," he said. "Thank you for your help." We hung up and I went inside to make supper. I sat outside on the deck for a few minutes. I went back inside the cabin and sat in my La-Z-Boy chair. I needed to put my leg up and rest.

I could hear the traffic up and down the highway. All I could think about was finding that man. Why did I have to get lost? How long was he there and who did this? I had so many questions I wanted answers to. I hoped they found him and didn't give up.

I went outside at 8 p.m. and watched the stars. It was getting darker much earlier now and the weather was cooler in the evening. I loved the breeze blowing through the windows at night. The cabin felt so nice and fresh, and I got a better sleep when it wasn't so stuffy. I went to bed and hoped to get a better sleep than last night.

I tossed and turned, but managed to get a few hours' sleep. I left and went to my course. The day was long, but I got through it. I left to go home and there was a traffic accident, and everything was tied up. The cars were bumper to bumper and not moving. I managed to turn around and head in the other direction. I saw a few more cars turn around and head my way. I didn't want to be lined up for hours. I was tired and sore. I just wanted to get home and relax.

**AFTER TURNING AROUND, I** saw a man running down the street, being chased by another man. I watched for a minute and saw the first man get into a black car that was parked around the corner. The man that was following him lost him and didn't know where he went. I rolled my window down and asked the man what happened.

"I was robbed and tried to catch the guy, but I lost him," said the man. I told him I just saw him get into a little black car and leave. I gave him the make and model and told him to call the police. "Thank you," he said, and I left and headed home. "I would have followed him if I had known the situation at the time."

I got home and made supper. It was a beautiful day, and the sun was shining. I wasn't very hungry, so I just made a salad. It was too hot to eat. I was thirsty and needed a cold drink. After supper, Officer Burns called.

"I don't have good news. We were unable to find the man or any indication he was there. My men searched for two days straight and had no luck. We must call off the search. I'm sorry to have to tell you this."

I said, "I was so sure they would have found him. I wish I could have stayed there and got help, but there was no cell service. I had to leave to try to call, and that's when I got lost. I'm glad you tried and hopefully he gets found." Officer Burns said goodbye and we hung up.

I was thinking of the man tied to the tree and what he must have gone through. It was sad to see him like that, covered in blood and half-dressed. I hoped they found him before they called off the search.

I went to bed and all I could think about was the guy tied to the tree. I wished they had found him. I wouldn't give up hope. I would love to go back and try to find him myself when I felt better. I'm not sure if that was a good idea or if I would even know where to look. I wouldn't want to get lost again.

I continued going to my courses and getting good marks. I would be done the courses in two more weeks. I would be so happy when they were done. The other students keep to themselves and that's fine with me. I just want to be able to get this done and concentrate on getting a high mark. I have a job waiting for me when I'm done these two courses. I need to finish with high marks to make this happen. I spend almost every night with my book open and study everything I learnt that day. I will be glad when the final day comes, as I write my exam.

My knee started to feel better, and my scrapes and cuts were healing fast. I kept thinking about going back to try to find the guy I'd seen tied to the tree. I knew he was there somewhere, and I couldn't just leave him there. I would do things a little differently this time. I would take a compass and a friend to help look. A couple of people looking would be better than one. It was eating at me that he was still there, somewhere deep in the woods.

Finally, the day had come that I wrote my last exam. I studied all night and don't think I slept at all. I was pumped to get this done. I had aced the last few tests I wrote, so was thinking positive today. I got ready and gathered up all my notes and books and headed into my class. I got to class early and sat and went over a few notes. There were a couple other students sitting down, studying. Ken, the teacher, was sitting at his desk. He was a tall, slim man with short brown hair. After a few minutes when everyone was at their desks, Ken walked around and handed us our final exam. "Good luck, and take your time," said Ken. "You have until 2:00 to finish, so don't rush. Look it over first before you start."

I read over the papers and went back to the first page and started writing. I knew it was going to take a while to finish. I took my time. The classroom was quiet, and everyone was writing. After almost three hours, I was finished. I looked it over and was happy with my answers. I got up, and brought it to Ken, who was sitting at his desk, reading. "It was nice having you in my class and I will see you on Monday between nine and two to get your final mark," said Ken. He laughed and said, "Have a great weekend and don't fall over any more banks."

I said, "I don't plan on it, but you never know what will happen in the woods. "

I left and went to treat myself to a late lunch. It was a nice, sunny day, and I didn't want to have to cook when I get home. I just wanted to sit on the deck and relax. I brought my lunch home and sat outside to eat. It was nice to listen to the birds and animals in the distance and the noise of traffic on the highway. This was what I called living in the woods.

Well, I had all weekend pacing the floor and worrying about my final mark. I had to wait until Monday, so I needed to keep busy. I was thinking an adventure would be nice to go on. I couldn't help but think about going back to find the guy on the tree. I needed to find him. I didn't think I could sleep another night knowing he was out there in the woods, all alone. I was wondering if my friend and neighbour would go with me tomorrow to try to find him. I just hoped they didn't think I was crazy when I told them why we were going in the woods.

I called my neighbour and my friend about going on an adventure tomorrow. They were both busy and couldn't go. "Call me again another time," said Bella. "I would have loved to go If I didn't already have plans."

I said, "I will call again. Take care and have a good weekend."

I sat home and enjoyed my evening making a few phone calls and catching up with friends. I decided to go back to the trail in the woods to see if I could fine the guy on the tree. He was on my mind, and I wouldn't sleep until he was found. I called Officer Burns to let him know I would be going back in the woods tomorrow to look for him. "I am not getting any sleep, he is on my mind night and day," I said.

"Let me call you back in a few minutes," said Officer Burns.

I went outside to sit on the deck to get some fresh air while I waited for him to call. The sky was getting dark, and I could hear the animals in the distance. After a few minutes, my phone rang. It was Officer Burns.

"I HAVE AN OFFICER I am going to send with you tomorrow,"
said Officer Burns. "Her name is Sandy, and she has been working
with us for a couple of years. She reminds me a lot of you. She has
so much energy and likes to see the results. It will be great for you
two to get to know each other for when you come work with us.
You will be seeing a lot of each other on different cases. Are you
able to meet at the station tomorrow morning at ten? Sandy will be
here and ready to go. You can both go in the squad car. "I can be
there for ten," I said and thanked him for letting me do this.

Officer Burns said, "I hope you can find him so he can be at
peace. We need to find who did this."

I knew I wasn't going to sleep, so I sat outside until after midnight. I went in to get a few hours' sleep. My window was open,
and a breeze was blowing through the cabin. I woke up at 2 a.m.
to the loud sound of something hitting the floor. It was a half-
filled plastic water bottle that blew off the dresser from the breeze.
I guess the breeze was stronger than I'd thought. I fell back asleep
until 7 a.m. I must have been tired. I got up and went on the deck
with my coffee. This was the day I got to go back in the woods and
try to find the guy I'd found tied to the tree. I went inside at 8:30
and packed a few sandwiches and some snacks. I was going to be

prepared this time in case we get lost again. Not that I wanted that to happen after the last time. I had everything ready to go, but just needed to get dressed. I drove to the police station to meet Sandy, who was going to be joining me today.

It was sunny but a little breezy, which was nice. My windows were down, and I was listening to country music. I got to town and parked my car at the police station. I went inside and Officer Burns was at the desk. "Good morning," said Officer Burns. "Let's go to my office for a minute. Sandy will be joining us in about ten minutes. She is just going over a case from last night."

"I wrote my final exam and will be getting my mark on Monday," I said to Officer Burns.

"This is great news," said Officer Burns. "Once we get your mark, we can get you on our team."

Sandy entered and introduced herself. "Hi, I am Sandy," she said.

I stood up and said, "Pleased to meet you," and introduced myself as Jill.

"Pleased to meet you, Jill. We have a full day ahead of us by the sounds of things," said Sandy.

I said, "We sure do, but let's hope it's worth the trip. I hope you packed an overnight bag."

"I heard what happened to you," said Sandy. "We got this. I don't plan on spending a night in the woods."

We left and went outside. I stopped at my car on the way and grabbed my backpack and put on my runners. I even took a hoody, just in case. We got in the squad car and headed on the highway. I kind of directed Sandy which way to go. Sandy was about my size but about ten years younger. She was athletic and had short brown hair. Sandy had been on the job for a total of twelve years. She had done some undercover work and enjoyed it. I mentioned I had just finished my courses and was waiting for my final marks. "Officer Burns has filled me in all about you."

"All good, I hope," I laughed.

"He has nothing but respect and good things to say about you. He even said you remind him of me."

We drove on the busy highway until I saw the turnoff. I pointed and said, "Turn left." We turned off the highway and headed in the direction of the trail. We met a few vehicles along the way. As we got to the parking lot, we could see people standing around and so many cars. We parked and got out. We grabbed our backpacks and headed down the trail.

I went down the narrow trail first, hoping to remember the direction where I had gone before. We walked and walked, but nothing was looking familiar. We saw people heading in different directions, but most of them stayed on the trail with the arrows. I thought there must be some sort of lookout where you could take pictures. We took a few different trails, but found nothing. Then I noticed a rock I had stopped at. Now I knew I was going in the right direction. "I remember stopping at this rock," I told Sandy. "I'm just not sure where I went after this, so I guess we will just have to keep going. The trail is not the trail that had arrows on it for people to follow. That is probably why nobody heads in this direction. It could be the reason the guy wasn't found yet." We walked and walked over the dry leaves and twigs. The sound was loud as we walked along the trail. We finally stopped and took a break. We sat on the ground and had a drink of water.

"Does anything look familiar?" Sandy asked. "Do you think we are going in the right direction? "

I wasn't sure, but I knew I had seen the rock when I was here. I just hoped we found the guy. I couldn't imagine him being here for so long and not found yet. We continued walking, stepping on broken branches crushing beneath our feet. The sound of dry leaves crunched as we walk. We could smell the fresh air and the wildflowers. The birds were chirping and the sound of people was in the distance. We must have been there for a couple of hours by then and still no sign of the guy.

We stopped at a small open area we found, just to have a snack. I had packed snacks and fruit. We ate an apple and a granola bar. Sandy had some dry berries and veggies in her backpack that we enjoyed. After we finished eating, we packed up and continued trying to find the guy strapped to the tree. It seemed like we were going farther into the woods. "I know he is here somewhere," I told Sandy. "We need to continue walking. I'm sure we will find him. We *must* find him. This isn't right for him to be out here like this."

Sandy agreed and said, "Think positively, and we will do our best to locate him."

It was hot and the bugs were bad. We walked and walked for hours, and still nothing. There were no signs of the guy. Sandy looked at me and said, "Which way do you think we should go?" There were three different trails to take, and we had to choose one, but didn't want to split up.

"I think we should go right," I said.

"OK," said Sandy. "Let's go right."

We made our way to the right and headed on the trail. After walking for about fifteen minutes, I noticed an old tin can I had seen before. It was off the trail, but I knew I had seen it when I was there the last time. I said, "Sandy, this is the way. I saw that old can before." She was excited and said, "Let's keep going and hope we find him." At this point, we were both walking faster, but it was getting so hot. We stopped and had a drink of water and kept going.

We walked through the narrow trail, getting scrapes from the thorn bushes and twigs along the way. It would all be worth it if we found him. We needed to find him. We walked for another hour through the bush. I looked up, and I could see the tree from a distance. I ran and said, "There he is." Sandy and I ran toward the tree until we were standing in front of it. She couldn't believe her eyes. She was shocked at what she was witnessing in front of her. This guy was so badly beaten and there was so much dried blood all over him and the ground. Sandy went over and looked in the pockets of his jeans to see if he had any ID. Unfortunately, he didn't have anything. He wasn't wearing a shirt or shoes. He was wrapped around the tree, tied and barefoot.

We stood there and tried our cellphones, but no service. We had to get help, but we were so far in the woods. "One of us needs to stay here, and one of us needs to go get help," said Sandy.

"I can stay, if you want to try to walk until you get service," I said. " If you go up higher, you might be able to make a call."

Sandy said, "That's a good idea and I can get them to follow the smoke signal to find us. I brought smoke locators to help with finding the location. Once I get service and make the call, I will come back, and we can set one off."

Sandy headed out and I stayed with the body on the tree. It was creepy staying there alone. I sat on the ground and drank some water. I took a few pictures and walked around. I thought maybe there might be something in the nearby woods that might be connected to this case. It was very dry and the leaves and brush beneath my feet were crunchy. I didn't want to go too far in the woods and end up lost. It was so hot, and I was alone in the woods with a body tied to a tree. I wanted to see if I could find anything connected to this case.

I walked around the area and found a stick that was covered in blood. There were a few cigarette butts and an empty roll of tape near the body. I took pictures and left everything where it was. I continued walking around the bushes to try to find something— anything—that would help us with this case. I wished I had some type of flags to mark the spot where the items were. I broke some large sticks and stood them in the ground whenever I found something that could be tied to the case.

Sandy had been gone for over an hour. I hoped she could get service and make a call for help. I walked to the opposite side of the woods. I made my way through the bushes in hopes of finding more evidence. The woods were dry, and the leaves and brush were crunchy as I walked. In the distance, I could see a shoe. I went over to find a man's white runner. It had blood on it. I took a picture and continued looking through the bushes. I knew the other shoe was there somewhere. I wanted to find it if I could. I looked around and came across a grey T-shirt, covered in dry blood. It looked like there was a pool of blood by the T-shirt. I thought: *Maybe this is where he was beaten and then dragged to the tree.* I took several pictures and left the items where they were. I put tall sticks in the ground, near the items, to help with the investigation. The police would need to come and bag everything and go over the entire area in case anything was missed.

I looked, but never found the other shoe. I didn't want to go too far in the woods. The shoe could have been thrown farther in the bush. I was sure the police would find it when they searched. Two hours had passed and still no sign of Sandy. I went back to the area where the body was. I could hear something in the distance, so I went in the bush and hid. I wanted to make sure it was Sandy and not someone coming back to the body. I didn't hear anyone talking. I could hear the crunching of leaves as the walking got closer to the area I was in. I was hoping it was Sandy making her way back to me to tell me help was on the way.

After a few minutes, I could see someone wearing a blue baseball cap. I knew then it wasn't Sandy. As he got closer, I could see a tall white male wearing jeans and a white T-shirt. I was hiding quietly in the bush. I didn't move a muscle. I watched as the guy walked over to the body and said, "You got what you deserve." All I kept thinking was that Sandy needed to get back there before this guy found me. I had no way to warn her. The guy then started in the other direction, looking through the woods. I was thinking he'd come back to collect any evidence that might have been left behind. I could hear the crunching sound as he walked. Every once and a while, the sound stopped. I could see him bend down as if he was picking something up. I kept thinking, *Sandy, please get back here.* I didn't want this guy to find me hiding in the woods. I was scared if I moved, he would hear me. It was quiet, so any movement sounded loud. I could hear his every step as he walked around. I heard ever twig break as he stepped on it.

I decided to go farther in the woods as quietly as I could. I tried to backtrack to the other side Sandy had headed in. I wanted to try to see if she was anywhere near us. I slowly made my way around the area without being seen. I crouched down and walked as quietly as possible. I knew he was collecting anything he could find. As I got to the other side, I found a large rock. I climbed up to see if there was any sign of Sandy. I couldn't see or hear anything. All I kept thinking was, *I hope she didn't get lost.* I needed her to get back here fast. I needed to warn her that we had company. I didn't want this guy to leave, or we may never find him. I did manage to get a few pictures of him. After about fifteen minutes, I could hear a noise coming toward me. I crouched down so I wasn't seen but could still hear the noise getting closer and closer. As the noise of breaking twigs and feet crunching leaves, I finally realized, it was Sandy. I didn't want to yell, so I started toward her. "Sandy. Over here," I said quietly. She stopped and came toward me.

"What are you doing over here?" she asked.

"I was walking around the area trying to find evidence, and a guy showed up. He went over to the guy tied to the tree and said, 'You got what you deserved.'

"I hid in the woods and quietly made my way out, to try to find you. He is still there walking through the woods. I think he might have come back to look for any evidence that might have been left behind. He is walking around the wooded area."

"I have help coming," said Sandy. "I had to walk several miles to get cell service. We need to get back to the area and find this guy. There will be a helicopter coming in about an hour to find our location. I need to send a smoke signal, so they can locate us. But first things first. I need to get to this guy and arrest him. I will need you to hide in the area as we get closer, so you don't get hurt. I have a weapon and you don't."

We quietly made our way back to the area. We could see from a distance where the body was. There were no signs of the other guy. We stood quietly and listened for any sounds that might indicate he was still there. Finally, we could hear twigs breaking and leaves crunching. He was close. "Stay here and duck down. I am going to get closer and find this guy."

Sandy started heading toward the area. I was watching from a short distance. I was ready in case she needed me. Not sure what I would do, but I was ready to jump in. I could see Sandy making her way through the woods in behind. Finally, I could hear her say, "This is the police. Stop where you are and get down on the ground." The guy was looking around and finally saw Sandy. She had her gun drawn and told him again, "Stop where you are and get down on the ground!" The guy slowly dropped to the ground and went down face first. She went over and put handcuffs on him.

He yelled, "What did I do?"

"I am taking you in for questioning in this murder," said Sandy. I made my way down now that it was safe. I could hear Sandy reading him his rights. He continued saying, "I didn't do anything."

"We will figure it out at the station," Sandy said and told him to stay sitting on the ground. She stood up and set off the smoke bomb so the helicopter could find us. We were in the woods a long way and may never be found. After about thirty minutes, we could hear the helicopter in the distance.

There was an open area for them to land. We now had a suspect in connection to this murder. We were both happy when we could see the helicopter. After a few minutes, the helicopter landed in an open area near where we were. I made my way over and Sandy stayed with the guy in handcuffs. There was an officer on the helicopter. He was a tall, dark-haired man. He introduced himself and we made our way over to where Sandy was. As he got closer, he asked Sandy who she had in handcuffs. After explaining the situation, she escorted him to the helicopter. "I need to get him back to the station so we can get to the bottom of this. I will take him in and get the helicopter to bring me back to finish up here." Sandy pointed to me and said, "You can stay here, and I will be back. We will need to take the squad car back to the station."

I stayed behind with the officer as he walked around and collected any evidence he could find. I helped him find and bag items of interest that were in the nearby area. After about an hour, we could hear the helicopter in the distance. After it landed, Sandy got out with another officer.

"These two officers are going to take over and we can make our way back to the squad car before it gets dark," said Sandy. She laughed and added, "We don't want to have to spend a night in the woods."

I said, "We certainly don't."

We left and headed toward the car. We tried as best as we could to follow back the way we came. Sandy had a good sense of direction, unlike me. After about two hours, we were back at the car. It was quite the hike back. We didn't take the time to stop; we just kept going and going.

We stood by the car and had a drink of water. "What a day this turned out to be," said Sandy. "I am glad we got to go back and find the guy. I couldn't get much sleep thinking about him out there all alone. Now to get some closure and find out who did this horrible crime. I guess we will be working together from time to time."

"I must go to the school on Monday to get my final mark. I worked so hard to get where I am today and hope it paid off."

"Think positively. I'm sure you did good," said Sandy.

**WE LEFT THE AREA** and headed to the station. The windows were down, and the wind was blowing through. The traffic was flowing heavily on the highway on the way into town. We talked all the way to the station. I found out Sandy had no family in town and was a workaholic. I told her I lived in a tiny cabin in the woods and absolutely loved it. As we approached the station, we could see an ambulance by the front door. We parked and got out and made our way into the station. Sandy asked the secretary at the front desk what was going on. She was told that the janitor had slipped on water and fell and hit her head.

I stayed for a few minutes inside the station and then told Sandy I was going to head home if she didn't need me. "You must be tired. If I need you for anything, I will be in touch," said Sandy. "I will be here filling out paperwork for a few hours. Have a good night and get some rest." I said goodbye and headed to my car.

I drove through town and picked up supper to take back to the cabin. I just wanted to sit outside and relax. It was getting dark, and I just wanted to get home. I sat out on the deck until about 8:00. I was tired, so I went inside to watch TV. I must have fallen asleep watching TV. I woke at 11:15. I got ready for bed and climbed in for a good night's sleep. I opened the window to let the fresh air in.

It was a beautiful Sunday morning, and I could feel the breeze coming through the open window. The sun was out, and the birds were chirping. I wanted to spend the day exploring around the property and clean up the yard. I sat out on the deck with my coffee and enjoyed the breeze, the smell of the wildflowers in the air, and the sound of the traffic on the highway. I was thinking about tomorrow and hoping I passed my final exam. I just wanted to keep busy and not think about going to my class tomorrow and getting my mark.

I spent the day around the outside of the cabin. It was a beautiful day to walk around and pick up garbage. I lit the firepit and burnt what I could find laying around the yard. It is about 3:00, when my phone rang. It was Sandy.

"Hello," she said.

"How are you doing?" I said.

"I am doing fine, just outside cleaning the yard. Are you able to stop in the station tomorrow after you get your final mark?" said Sandy.

"I sure can," I said. "I should be there about 10 a.m."

"Perfect," said Sandy. "I will see you then."

I went inside and got cleaned up and made supper. I was excited about going to school tomorrow to get my mark. I am not sure why Sandy wanted me to stop by the station, but I guess I will find out when I get there. I turned the news on, then watched a show until bedtime.

I got ready on this sunny Monday morning. It was time to head to town and get my final mark. I left my house at 9:30 to head out on the busy highway. I stopped to get a coffee when I got to town. I parked and went inside to get my mark. I walked up the stairs and down the hallway. I met a few of my classmates walking in the hall. I went inside and over to the desk where Ken was sitting. He said, "You did great. I am very proud of you, and you should be proud of yourself. You had the highest mark in the entire class. Your final mark was 94 percent."

"I was so happy I passed and with such a high mark," I said.

"You worked hard, and you deserve the mark you got," said Ken. "I wish you all the luck in the future and nothing but the best. He handed me my exam and I left the class. I needed to go get my mark from my self-defence course. I headed down the hall and made my way in the other classroom. The teacher was there but was with other students. I waited a few minutes, and my name was called. I was handed my paper and I left. I went outside the class and stopped to look at my paper. I had a 91 percent as my final mark. I was happy with that.

I went down the hall to the stairs and headed out to my car. I had to go to the station to meet with Sandy. I also wanted to stop to see Officer Burns when I got to the station. I needed to give him a copy of my final exams.

I got to the station and went inside. I went to see Officer Burns and gave him the good news. As I walked down the hall to his office, he was walking toward me. He said, "Good morning. What brings you here?"

I said, "I am here to see you and Sandy. Here are my final marks, I thought you might want to look at them." I handed the papers to him, and he said, "Wow, you really did good. I will make a copy and get these back to you and then we need to talk." He told me to head to his office and wait there for him. After about ten minutes, he came in and sat at his desk. Sandy filled me in on the discovery of the body in the woods.

"I am glad you both went and found him. I also heard she arrested a man at the scene. I haven't had a chance to question him yet, but I will be doing that today," said Officer Burns. I said, "I am so glad we were able to find him. I couldn't imagine him out there another night."

After talking for a few more minutes, Sandy entered the room and took a seat. "I'm glad you could make it today," she said. "How did you do on your finals?" I handed them to her, and she had a big smile.

"Good for you," she said. "Very well deserved. Now we can get down to business. I guess you are wondering why we wanted you here today. Well, we are going to interview and question the guy we found near the body in the woods. We want you to see how this is done and how things are done by the book. This is a good way to learn, by watching it firsthand."

"I would be happy to be a part of this. Thank you for including me."

All three of us left and headed down the hallway. Sandy took me in a room with a window that could see in the interrogation room. She said, "You can see him, but he can't see you. This is where you will watch us in action. So far, he said his name is Kevin and he never said anything else. We are going in there to see what he has to say about why he was there near the body, collecting evidence. We want you to observe and see how this is done. We hope he will tell us what happened.

"Hi, Kevin. I am Sandy and this is Officer Burns," she said. "We want to talk to you about what happened to the guy in the woods. Do you know what happened to him?"

"I didn't do anything," said Kevin.

"Then tell us why you were there collecting evidence and why you said, 'You got what you deserve.' Right now, we are charging you with murder, unless you can tell us what happened. You will be serving life in prison if you don't tell us the truth." Kevin spoke, saying, "I didn't touch him. He got what he deserved but not from me. I wasn't there at the time but was asked to go back and collect any evidence I could find."

"Who did this, Kevin?" asked Officer Burns. "You need to tell us, or we can't help you. You will be going to jail for this horrific crime."

"Do you want to go to jail, Kevin?" said Sandy.

"No," said Kevin. "But he got what he deserved."

"Tell us why he got what he deserved," said Officer Burns. "What did he do that he deserved a beating like that and then tied to a tree?"

"It wasn't me," said Kevin.

"Well, tell us what you know so we can help you," said Sandy. "We need you to tell us the truth about what happened."

"His name was Greg. He raped my friend's thirteen-year-old daughter. Now tell me he didn't get what he deserved. I am not talking anymore. I am done talking and want to make a phone call."

"When did this happen?" said Sandy. "You need to tell us who did this, so we can help them. If you protect someone, you will go to jail for them."

"Is this what you want?" said Officer Burns.

"No," said Kevin. "But if it was your daughter, what would you do?"

"I would probably feel like doing the same thing, but I would have to let the law deal with it," said Officer Burns.

"Well, we all know how good the law is in protecting the accused," said Kevin. "The victim never has a chance and must live with it all their life."

"Kevin, give me the name of the person who did this so we can help him," said Officer Burns. "If he doesn't come forward soon, it doesn't look good for him. Please, let us help him."

"Who did this, Kevin?" said Sandy.

A few hours went by, and Kevin wasn't giving the name of the person responsible for this crime. "We tried everything," said Sandy. "This is not looking good for Kevin," said Officer Burns. "We will arrest him on murder charges and maybe he will give us the name of the person responsible. I'm sure he doesn't want to go to jail for a crime he didn't commit.

"Kevin," said Officer Burns, "we are charging you with first-degree murder in the death of Greg. Do you really want to go to jail for a crime you didn't commit?"

"You must have family that needs you," said Sandy.

"You can't arrest me if I didn't do it," said Kevin.

"We can and we are," said Officer Burns, "unless you give us a name. We want to help your friend, and this is the only way."

"I don't think your friend will want you to go to jail for him," said Sandy. "Give us his name so we can help him."

"Would you like a phone call, Kevin?" said Sandy.

"Yes, I would," said Kevin. Officer Burns left the room and went to get a phone for Kevin to call his friend. After a few minutes, Officer Burns returned with a phone and handed it to Kevin. "You can make your one phone call now," said Officer Burns.

"I will make my call if you both leave the room," said Kevin. We both got up to leave and said, "We will be back in five minutes." We were hoping Kevin would call the friend who did this crime. The recording was still on in the room so we would be able to hear the conversation.

Kevin made his phone call. "I have been arrested," he said. "I was in the woods gathering up evidence and the police showed up and arrested me. They are charging me with murder if I don't talk. I am scared and don't know what to do." The conversation was silent for a few seconds, then we could hear Kevin say, "Are you sure? The police said they would help you if you turned yourself in. When the judge hears the story of what Greg did to your daughter, you might not get a lot of time in jail. OK, I will tell the police you are turning yourself in. I will see you in half an hour. I'm sorry this had to happen."

Kevin hung up the phone and sat there for a few minutes. Officer Burns and Sandy went back in the room. "The guy's name that did this is Mark. He is on his way in. He is turning himself in," said Kevin. "He doesn't want me to go to jail for a crime I didn't commit."

"Thank you," said Officer Burns. "You are doing the right thing by reaching out to your friend and having him turn himself in." Sandy asked Kevin if he would like some food and a drink. Kevin calmly said, "I would love something to eat and a coffee, please. Is there any way I can go out for a smoke?"

"I can take you," Sandy said. "Let's go out the back door where it's a smoking area and there is a bench there to sit at."

Kevin and I made our way outside to the smoking area while Officer Burns went out front to order food and a get a coffee for Kevin. "I knew this was going to be a stressful day," said Sandy. Kevin broke down and said he felt so bad that Mark's daughter had to go through what she did. "How could Mark do this to her? He has been a friend of the family for so long. How does someone do this? She is so young and now she is hurting," said Kevin. "My friend Mark is a very good person and a fantastic dad. He is a family man, and this is destroying him. I honestly think I would have done the same thing if it were my daughter. People snap and don't even realize what they are doing until it is too late." I just listened to Kevin and let him talk.

"He was keeping everything inside and this is his way of dealing with it," said Sandy. I'm sure it's a huge weight off his shoulders for telling the truth."

Officer Burns came out where we were and said the food was there and so was Mark. We went inside to the room and let Kevin have lunch and a coffee. Mark was in the other interrogation room telling his side of the story to Officer Burns.

Sandy came in the room where I was watching Kevin tell his side of the story. It was interesting to watch and see how things worked in the real world. I was sure Kevin and Mark were good friends by the way Mark stepped up to the plate and turned himself in. He obviously didn't want Kevin to go to jail for a crime he didn't commit. Mark was now in the other room giving a full confession of what had happened. "What did you think of this?" said Sandy.

"I think it was very interesting to listen to. I'm glad I was able to watch this and learn from this."

"Well, this is going to be a long night," said Sandy. "I will be in touch with you and let you know how things worked out. Mark will be arrested after giving his statement."

I said, "Thank you for giving me the opportunity to be a part of this."

Sandy said, "It was my pleasure."

**I LEFT THE STATION** after having been there for several hours. Now I understood how it could take hours and hours to get to the truth. I drove through town on this nice, sunny day. I went to the grocery store and picked up some chicken to barbecue when I got home. I wanted to get home and sit outside on the deck for a while. I opened my windows and cranked the music all the way home. The traffic was heavy, so I took my time.

I put my groceries away and went out on the deck and listened to the birds. It was such a peaceful day. I am glad to be home to enjoy the rest of it. I started the barbecue and made a salad to have with my chicken. After supper, I put a fire on in the firepit. I sat outside until about 9 p.m. It is such a beautiful evening. I went inside and watched TV until midnight. The cabin was stuffy, so I opened the window and went to bed.

I woke up after having had a great sleep. It felt weird not to get up and go to class. I was so glad that my classes were finished. I felt free again and was looking forward to working with the police on some cases. I sat outside wondering what to do that day. I was thinking of going on an adventure somewhere. I cleaned up my dishes, and got dressed and ready for an adventure. I packed the cooler and headed to my car. I drove to the highway and headed toward some dirt roads. I had my windows down and the music on. I turned off a road I had never been down before, or at least that's what I thought. I go down so many different roads, it's hard to remember which ones I have taken before. I liked to explore and see what I could find. There wasn't much traffic today, so it was easy to take my time and park and take pictures of the scenery. I liked to look for old, abandoned farmhouses. It was nice to see how people lived back in the day compared to today. I got a sense of that when I went inside these farmhouses and old homes. I found and saw things that sometimes I didn't even know what they were. I took so many pictures of unique things. I liked to walk around the property and look in old sheds and barns. I followed the road almost to the end and spotted an old barn. I didn't see a house, other than a small, boarded-up shack. Well, I guess that's where they could have lived. Houses were smaller back in the day. Families were big and houses were small. I knew that was how I grew up.

I pulled up to the gate, which had an old, rusted lock on it. I got out of my car and, as I approached the gate, I could see the lock wasn't locked. It was just through the old, rusted, heavy chain. I took the lock out from the chain, and opened the gate just enough to get my car through. I drove up the long, wide driveway, hoping nobody saw me. Although there wasn't anyone around, I still had to be careful not to get caught on private property. I didn't notice any signs around the area or at the gate.

I got to the old, boarded-up shack. I walked up the wooded steps. They were rotten and wobbly as I made my way to the top. The rails on both sides were hanging off. I had to be careful not to fall through the steps. There were holes in the wood and large nails sticking up. As I got to the old, boarded-up wooden door, I could see inside, through a crack. I wanted to get inside and look around. The roof looked like it was falling in. I tried to pry the door open but didn't have any luck. There was no lock on it, so I kept pushing it with my hip and shoulder. Finally, after struggling a few minutes, the door was open. It was dusty and had spiderwebs all over the place. I slowly went inside to look around. It smelt bad. There was a small entrance as you entered. To the right, I could see a sink and a few cupboards in the kitchen. The doors were hanging off the painted dark brown cupboards. There was an old woodstove with a pot on it. There was a broken rocking chair off to the side.

I walked in a little farther down the narrow hallway. At the end of the hall was a little room. I had to cover my face as much as I could from the strong smell. It had an old wrought iron bed frame with a stained mattress. There were three other mattresses on the floor piled up on top of one another. The window was boarded up. There were holes through the floors as I walked. I had to be careful not to fall though the floor. I found an old wooden chest with chains on it. It was covered in dust and the chains were rusted. I couldn't wait to see what was inside this wooden chest. There was no lock on it, so it would be easy to open. I lifted the heavy rusted chains off so I could see inside.

As I slowly opened the chest, I saw a dirty pink blanket sticking out of a garbage bag. It looked dirty and dusty and smelt bad. It might be just the closed-up shack that smelt so bad. I opened the bag and was shocked at what I saw next. There were human remains of what looked like a baby. It was wrapped in a pink blanket and was just skeleton remains. I could tell it was a baby wrapped up. I stood back and thought: *What did I just find?* I needed to call Officer Burns and let him know what I'd found. *Who'd left a baby here in a wooden chest wrapped up? How could anyone do this?* I continued taking pictures of everything I saw. I looked around the house and didn't find anything else except a few old books. I headed outside and made a call to Officer Burns.

He couldn't believe what I had come across. "I will be on my way soon," said Officer Burns. "Just stay there and wait for me." I told him I would be there when he arrived. I gave him directions and he said he would be about an hour.

I walked around the property outside and made my way to the barn. I wanted to see what was inside of it. The doors were open and hanging off the hinges. There were a few old, rusted bike parts against the wall. I found an old wooden wagon and water buckets as I entered the barn. I saw a loft with an old wooden ladder leaning against the rafters. There was nothing interesting in there, so I went back outside to look around the property. I went behind the barn to where I saw a couple of old, rusted cars. It was obvious they had been sitting there for many years. The hoods were up, and they were full of brush and rust. The windows and lights were smashed on them. The seats were ripped and there was glass all over the place. I walked around until I heard a car pull up the driveway. I made my way down to where Officer Burns and Sandy were standing outside the little boarded-up shack.

"I found the little body inside in a wooden chest," I told them. We went inside the house, with me leading the way to where the body was. "Be careful," I said, as we walked. The floors were caving in and there were holes throughout.

"The smell in here," said Sandy as she walked through the house. Officer Burns covered his face with his hands as he walked through to get to the room.

"There it is in the wooden chest," I said. "Just open it and you will see it."

"Wow," Officer Burns said, as he looked inside the old, dirty chest.

"Who and why would someone do this to a baby?" said Sandy. "This certainly looks like it's been here for quite some time." They both looked around and were convinced there was nothing else in the house that would help them with this case.

"We need to get this back to autopsy and see if we can somehow figure out. We will need to see who this property belongs to and that may help us identify this baby," said Officer Burns.

"Sandy," said Officer Burns, "could you please go around and get as many pictures of this house as you can? Take some of the room and the inside of the house as well as the outside and around the yard."

We went outside, carefully carrying the wooden chest with the remains inside. We talked for a few minutes and Officer Burns said he would be in touch as soon as he heard anything. He thanked me and asked Sandy if she was done taking pictures. "I am all done here," said Sandy. "I think I got enough pictures to try to figure this out."

I approached Sandy and asked her if they had any cases I would be working on in the future. "We have a big case we have been working on for a few months," said Sandy. "We will be getting you to work the case with us very soon. It's going to be an undercover case we will need you for."

"That's great news," I said. We said our goodbyes and I headed to the highway.

I headed home to the cabin. It had been a successful day and time to make supper and sit outside. There was still some light left in the day to enjoy. I hoped they could find out who lived in that old house and why that baby had been left there in an old chest.

So many things went through my mind. Was the baby stillborn or had a young teenager given birth, and this was their way of hiding it? It still didn't make it right to put a baby in a wooden box. I guess we never know what we will find in these old shacks and homes. Therefore, I loved to get out and explore.

I sat outside after I got back home. I grabbed a bottle of water and turned on the music. It was a bright, sunny day with birds chirping and traffic going up and down the highway. After about an hour, my phone rang. It was Sandy. "I am wondering if you happened to get any pictures today of the house we were at," said Sandy. "My camera, for some reason, didn't take very clear pictures. It could have been the lighting or the sunshine."

"I have several pictures I can give you. I took about 300 pictures today, so you are welcome to have them. I can bring them in tomorrow, and you can get them off my phone," I said.

"That would be great. I will see you tomorrow," said Sandy.

After talking to Sandy, I looked through my phone at all the pictures I'd taken. I had many pictures of the inside and all around the outside and the yard. My pictures seemed to be clear. I sat around until about 7 p.m. It was such a nice evening, and I didn't want to go inside. I went in long enough to make a salad and take it out on the deck. I sat and ate and listened to my music. At about 9 p.m., I went inside to watch TV. I was getting tired. I shut the TV off at midnight and went to bed.

I got up at about 7 a.m., and took my coffee outside on the deck. I sat until about ten and went in to get ready to go to the station with the pictures for Sandy. I didn't want to waste this beautiful day inside a police station. I wanted to be quick so I could go explore the dirt roads again. I packed a few things in my cooler and made my way into the station.

I got to the station at 11:15 and went to find Sandy. She was at her desk. I gave her my phone so she could get the pictures off it. After about twenty minutes, Sandy came and gave me my phone. "Thank you," said Sandy. "I have all the pictures I need."

**I LEFT THE STATION** and headed onto the highway in the opposite direction I usually went. It was a beautiful summer day with lots of sunshine. I stopped at a gas station to get gas and a cold drink. The station had several cars waiting to gas up. I waited about five minutes, then was finally able to get gas. I parked my car and went inside to grab a drink. I could hear two young guys talking about how easy it would be to rob one of these little stores. They were talking low, but I had good ears.

"I don't see any cameras in here," said the one guy.

"I don't either," said the other young guy.

I took notice as to what they were wearing and got a description of them both. I let on I didn't hear anything as I just looked the other way. They must have been about seventeen years old. Both white males, five foot ten. One had blondish hair and the other dark brown, curly hair. They both were wearing caps and jeans. I managed to look around and finally made my way to the till to pay for my drink and bag of plain chips.

I went to my car and waited to see if they would come out. I wanted to see if they had a vehicle there so I could get some pictures and a description of what they were driving. I was hoping to get a licence plate number just in case this place got robbed.

After about three minutes, the two young guys came out of the gas station. They both headed over to a small red Chev pickup truck. I immediately got a picture of the truck and the plate number. The two guys left and headed down the highway in the opposite direction I was headed.

I drove for about a half hour then came across a lookout sign. There were a few cars pulled over, looking, and taking pictures of the scenery. It was a beautiful lookout full of mountains and colours. I got out and took some pictures of the scenery. *What a beautiful site this is*, I thought. I stayed there for about ten minutes, taking pictures. Finally, I left the area and headed down the highway, yet once again.

I found a few gift shops along the way. I stopped at all of them, hoping to buy something unique. I spotted a shiny silver chain with a bright red stone. The stone was set in a black round base. It was the colour of my dad's birthstone, which was July.

"These are made by a local lady," said the owner of the shop. The little elderly lady behind the counter, said, "I have owned this shop for over forty years now, and it's about time to retire. My kids are grown and moved away now, so they don't want anything to do with taking this shop over. It will kill me to have to close the doors, but I don't have much choice. I am getting older, and my health is not the best. I lost my husband four years ago, and this is all I have left. We built this shop together and I have so many memories."

I said, "Well, you have a lovely little place and I wish you all the best." I paid for my beautiful necklace and left the shop. I made my way down the highway a little farther. It was getting late, and the traffic was heavy. I decided to turn around and head back toward my house. I didn't like to drive in the dark unless I needed to.

I had my windows open, and the music cranked as I drove down the open highway. *There is no better feeling than this,* I thought as I drove through this beautiful scenery. After a few minutes of listening to my music, the news came on. "We are asking the public to be

on the lookout for a small red pickup truck with two male suspects who are wanted in the questioning of a robbery at a gas station."
I immediately thought about the gas station I had just been to a short time before. This must be the two guys I'd overheard talking about robbing the place. They had a red pickup truck. I pulled over and made a call to Officer Burns.

"I think I might have some information on the robbery of the gas station that just came over the news," I said.

"I'm listening," said Officer Burns. "What can you tell me?"

"I was out on an adventure and decided to go to a gas station to gas up. As I was inside, I overheard two young guys talking about how easy it would be to rob this place. I went outside and got a few pictures of them and what they were driving. They got into a little red pickup truck and drove away."

"Did you happen to get the licence plate and a description of the two guys?" said Officer Burns.

"I did indeed," I said. I gave him the information of the guys and the licence plate of the truck. "Thank you so much for your help," said Officer Burns. "I'm sure this will help us locate these two guys and bring them in for questioning." We both hung up and I headed back on the highway.

I got home at about 7 p.m. The weather was still nice and sunny. I sat out on the deck for a few hours before I went inside and went to bed.

**I WOKE AT ABOUT** 6 a.m., to the sound of the birds chirping through my open window. The soft summer breeze was blowing through, and the smell of fresh air was amazing. I knew it was going to be a nice, sunny day. Now I had to decide what to do. I wanted to go explore around, but I also had work to do around the cabin. I sat on the deck for a few hours to start my day. I sipped my coffee and listened to the sound of the birds. I could hear the neighing of the horses next door, the dogs barking and the roosters crowing. *What a wonderful sound*, I thought to myself. *You wouldn't get to hear these sounds by living in town in a neighbourhood. This is so peaceful and relaxing.*

Today was the day I tried hard to get my work done outside so I had time to venture off somewhere down a dirt road. All I thought about was exploring and taking in the sights. Farmhouses, old barns, and whatever else I could find. Life is too short to sweat the small stuff. Get out there and live a little is what I tell people. After about three hours sitting on the deck, I went inside to get dressed. I worked around the yard for a couple of hours and got so much accomplished. I felt like now I deserved to go on an adventure and see what I could find.

I packed the cooler and called my friends Hope and Bella to see if they would like to join me exploring that day. They both said they would love to.

"Meet at my house in an hour," I told them. They both showed up an hour later and off we went. The three of us went in my car and headed down the highway. We never know where we might land, so we always try to pack the cooler and snacks. We drove for about fifteen minutes, and Bella said, "Look, turn down that road to the left."

"Let's see what's down there," Hope said, in her very low voice. "Yes, that's a good idea." I slowed down and turned onto the dirt road. We drove for a few minutes, then I pulled over to look down a long, narrow driveway.

"Look," I said. "It's an old, boarded-up farmhouse." We all got out of the car and went over to the locked gate. There were two large, rusted chained-up gates across the bottom of the driveway.

"Well, we can't drive up," said Bella, "but we can walk." Bella, Hope, and I headed up the long driveway. We could see the farmhouse as we got closer.

"This place looks like there hasn't been anyone living here for years," said Hope. "Well," said Bella, "let's look around and see what we can find." I spotted an old shed around the back of the house. I headed toward it to look inside. Bella and Hope went to look in the farmhouse. There were a few old cars around the back of the house and a few rusted bikes. I took a few pictures and went inside the shed. I walked around the dirty, cobwebbed shed. There were old, rusted tools and a large table against the back wall. There was a large white rusted deep-freeze against the other side of the shed. As I walked over to the deep-freeze, I felt a cold chill go down my back. The freezer has a large padlock on it.

I called Hope and Bella to see where they are. I wanted them to help me open the freezer. Bella answered her phone and asked where I was. I am around the back in an old shed. "Can you and

Hope come out here," I said with a tremble in my voice? "What's wrong", said Bella? "I found something here and I need your help to open it," I said.

"OK," said Bella. "Hope and I are headed out there now to help you. Come on, Hope. Jill needs our help in a shed in the backyard. She found something and needs us."

"Of course she did," said Hope. "She always finds something interesting. Let's go see what she found."

I waited a few minutes for Hope and Bella to join me in the shed. They both entered and came over to where I was standing. "What did you find," said Bella? "Look at this old freezer with the lock on it," I said. Doesn't it look suspicious to you guys? There is a large lock on it and that makes me want to look inside and see what's in there. "Well let's look around to see if we can find something to cut the lock off," said Hope. All three of us looked around the old dirty shed to see if we could find cutters.

"Look," said Hope, I found a little rusted hack saw."

"That might work," I said. "Hold the chain and I will try to saw through the lock. After a few minutes, its wasn't doing anything. "Here," said Bella, let me try. She chuckled and said," I'm stronger than both of you." Let me use some of my muscles. Hope and I held the chain and Bella worked the saw back and forth until the lock broke free. "There you go," said Bella. Its off, so now let's look inside.

All three of us were wondering what could be inside, so we all had to guess what we thought it could be." I think it's a freezer full of meat that has been left here for years," said Bella.

"It really stinks, so it must be something that went bad over the years," said Hope. "I think it is wild meat, like deer and moose."

"Well," I said, "I think you are both wrong. Why would someone put a lock and chain on a freezer and leave it out here in the middle of nowhere? I am guessing it is bodies, so stand back as I open the lid."

Both Bella and Hope laughed and said at the same time, "You are crazy to think it is dead bodies."

"Why would you even say that?" said Hope.

"Well, it's like this," I said. "Why would anyone lock a freezer and why does it smell so raunchy?"

"This freezer has been here unplugged for many years, by the look of it," said Hope.

"Well," I said, "let's open it and look inside." All three of us lifted the lid. The smell made us step back and take a breath.

"Oh, the stink," we said. Bella stepped back and was gagging. She started to vomit. Hope stood back and felt sick. They both said, "What is inside there?" There were plastic bags, filled to the top of the freezer. I went up a little closer to get a better look. I could see hair sticking out of the plastic bags. I knew now, this was a freezer full of bodies. Well, at least one that I could see. I didn't want to touch anything just in case there was any evidence or fingerprints anywhere. I told Hope and Bella that the freezer had at least one body in it. They couldn't believe what they were hearing.

"Are you sure?" said Hope.

"I am sure," I said. "I can see hair sticking out of a plastic bag. We need to go to my car, and I need to call the police. We can't touch anything. We just need to leave."

"Oh, don't worry," said Bella, "about me touching anything. I just want to get the heck out of here."

"Me, too," said Hope.

"Let's leave and never look back," they both said.

We walked down the driveway back to my car and had a drink of water. Both Bella and Hope felt sick to their stomachs. "How does this not bother you?" said Hope. "Oh, it does," I said. "But I need to focus and find out who did this." This was a huge discovery and people need to be held accountable for this. "There will be a huge investigation and the property will need to be analyzed for any evidence to help solve this case," I said. "Just give me a minute to call my friend and tell him about this." Hope and Bella walked around the car and shook their heads. I made my call to Officer Burns.

"Are you telling me you found a freezer with a body in it?" said Officer Burns.

"I did, and it could contain more. The freezer is full to the top and I saw hair sticking out of a plastic bag. The smell will make you sick," I said. "The freezer is in a shed behind an old farmhouse. I do have my two friends here with me now. We were just out on an adventure when we came across an old farmhouse. I went out back and found the shed. All three of us opened the freezer after breaking the lock."

"I will be there in half an hour with my crew to collect any evidence we can find. We will need to rope off the entire area and see what else we can find. Are you able to stay, but have your friends leave the area?" said Officer Burns.

"I can let them take my car if I can get a drive back home with someone."

"I can have someone take you back home when we are through," said Officer Burns. "I'm sure Sandy will be joining us too."

"Bring lock cutters for the locked gate at the end of the driveway," I said. "We had to park my car and walk up the driveway."

"OK," said Officer Burns.

I told Bella and Hope to head back to my place with my car. "I need to stay here and wait for the police to arrive," I said. "I will get a ride back home with someone after we are done." Hope and Bella looked white as ghosts.

"I don't know how you can do this for a living," said Hope.

"This is not something I would do," Bella said. "I will park your car and leave the keys in the barbecue on your deck."

I said, "Thank you," and they both left. I could see them drive down the dirt road as I waited for the police and team to arrive. I sipped my bottle of water and waited about fifteen minutes for the police to arrive on scene.

I could hear the cars coming up the dirt road. As they got closer, I could see the dirt in the air. I knew they were getting close. Four police cars final arrived where I was standing at the end of the driveway. Officer Burns got out of his cruiser. He had another officer cut the lock and we all made our way up the long driveway. We all got out, and I said, "The shed is over here behind the house."

We walked through the yard around the back of the house to get to the old shed. The yard had a couple of old cars and rusted wheels around the area. There was an old shed with no door on it. "It doesn't look like anyone lived here for quite some time," said Officer Burns.

I said, "Most of these old places have been abandoned for many years." I laughed and added, "That's why I like coming to them." Officer Burns grinned and we kept walking.

We got to the shed and went inside to look in the freezer. Officer Burns said, "I can smell it from here." He got closer and looked inside the old freezer. He put his hand over his mouth. "That's some nasty smell," he said with a grin. "Let's collect whatever we can from the area. Get some tarps down and start getting evidence bagged and labelled."

We walked around the area looking for anything else that could help with this case. We came across an old barrel that had ashes in it. Officer Burns called for another officer to come over with a tarp. "I want this emptied on a tarp and collect anything you might find," he told the young officer. Hours went by and tarps were on the ground as everything was collected. "We are going to be here for a while, Jill," said Officer Burns. "Did you want me to have an officer take you home so you can get some rest? It's been quite the day for you."

"No, I would like to stay if that's OK with you."

"Absolutely, you can stay. This is the real world and its best you see how things are done by the book. After we are done here, I have a case we need your help with. All your paperwork was approved for you to finally be able to work with us. We have been working on a case for several months now and need your help."

I said," I am excited to finally be able to work with you. I can't thank you enough for helping me and encouraging me to take the courses I needed to make this happen."

"It was my pleasure," said Officer Burns.

One of the officers came over to us and said, "There is a total of nine girls in the freezer. They collected clothing and a few purses that were stored under the shed in a garbage bag. We haven't found any remains other than what was in the freezer."

"Keep looking and collect as much as you can. We need to find out who did this," said Officer Burns. "I am going to head back to the office in an hour or so to try to figure out who lived here. This will help us find out why these ladies were murdered and hopefully who did it."

Officer Burns saw the coroner van pull in the yard and come up the driveway. He waved his arm and pointed in the direction of where the freezer of bodies was. He wanted the van as close as possible to be able to have all the bodies removed and taken back for examination.

"Good afternoon, gentleman," said Officer Burns as they got out of the van. "We have a total of nine bodies in a freezer. We will need this case to be put on the priority list, if possible. My team will continue searching the premises for any more evidence in this case. We will get the bodies loaded in the van and take them back to the lab."

"As soon as I get any information, I will call you," said one of the coroners.

"Thank you," said Officer Burns. "I really appreciate it."

After about twenty minutes, the nine bodies were loaded in the van and taken back to the lab to be analyzed. We looked around the yard and the house to see if there was anything we were missing." So many questions we needed answers to, but it's going to take time," said Officer Burns. I walked over to where Sandy was standing outside the shed. "Hi, "I said to Sandy. "Hi, Jill, how are you doing today?" she said with a half-smile. I was doing fine on an adventure until I came across these bodies. "My friends and I were out for a fun filled day until this happened," I said. "Well, you can never be happier finding nine bodies stuffed in a freezer," said Sandy with a grin. "No, I guess not," I said. "Therefore, life seems so interesting and makes me want to work in the field," I said to Sandy.

"Good," said Sandy. "We have a big case we need you to join us with. It's the one we talked about with the drugs and selling of teenage girls. We need to break this case before more girls get hurt."

"I am looking forward to it," I said with a smile.

The area was searched over and over, but nothing else was found. A few pieces of clothing and other personal items were bagged and taken into evidence. "Hopefully, this will give us a few clues to help us with solving this case," said Sandy. After a few more hours went by, Officer Burns approached me and said he would drive me home. "I must go to the station to work on this case," he said. "I will drive you home on the way. They are almost done here, so we can leave so I can get back and get started. The quicker I find out who lived here, the quicker I should have some answers. I'm sure these girls had family missing them. I will get Sandy to investigate missing girls as soon as we get conformation on an approximate time of death."

I said goodbye to Sandy and left with Officer Burns. We got on the highway at about 7 p.m. It was still daylight, and the sun was still out. "What a day this turned out to be," I said to Officer

Burns." I don't think my friends will want to come on anymore adventures with me."

He laughed and said, "Well, it wouldn't be an adventure if you didn't find interesting things. But then again, with you, it's always interesting."

I laughed and said, "I am looking forward to working the big case with you soon."

"Yes," said Officer Burns. "Give me a few days, and I will get you to come in and get briefed on what we are working on now. I said, "I can't wait to help and get in the field." We made idle chit chat on the drive to the cabin. "You will love working with Sandy," said Officer Burns. "She is a wonderful person who takes her job seriously and puts her heart and soul in each case she works on. She reminds me a lot of you."

**WE GOT TO THE CABIN,** where Officer Burns drove up my long driveway. We said goodbye and he drove to the station. I needed to go inside and get some food and a cold drink. I grabbed a bottle of water and went out to sit on the deck. I know it's going to be long days when I start working in the field. I called Bella and Hope to let them both know I was home. I didn't talk about anything we discovered today. I told them, it was an ongoing investigation and that was all I could say. I stayed outside for an hour enjoying the rest of my day. It was getting cool, so I went inside to make a sandwich and watch the news. I was glad to be back home. I couldn't help but think about those girls and what might have happened to them. I was glad we came across them in the freezer. I'm sure Officer Burns will get to the bottom of this as soon as he gets the information on time of death.

I went to bed at midnight after watching the news, while dozing off and on for a few hours in my chair. I was hoping tomorrow to head back to the area where the bodies were discovered. I wanted to see if they were done and if the area still roped off.

I woke off and on all night. My mind was racing, and I kept thinking of those girls in the freezer. Who were they and how did they get murdered? I have so many unanswered questions and wanted to see the result. I needed to know more and find out who was responsible for this hateful crime. I got up and went out on the deck with my morning coffee. The weather is sunny and not a cloud in the sky. I knew it is going to be a nice day for a drive. I finished a couple cups of coffee and went in to get ready to go. I packed my cooler and headed out the door. I made my way to the highway to go back to the farmhouse where the bodies were discovered yesterday.

It is a busy day on the highway as I drove a few miles down the road. The traffic is heavy, so I took my time and just listened to my music. I finally got to the road where I was about to turn down to get to the farmhouse. I can see a police car coming towards me. As it passed, I kept driving towards the farmhouse to see if anyone else was still on scene. As I approached the farmhouse, I made my way up the long driveway. I was greeted by an officer. "Excuse me, ma'am, but this area is off limits, and you will have to turn around," said the officer.

"Oh, I am Jill. I am the one who called this in yesterday," I said. "I work with Officer Burns, and I just came back to see if they were all finished here, but it looks like that's not the case."

"No," said the officer. "They found more bodies underneath a cellar that was attached to the farmhouse. Officer Burns is on his way as we speak. My name is Jake."

"I am Jill and pleased to meet you," I said," as I shook his hand. "I am just going to look around and I will wait for Officer Burns to arrive."

"That's fine by me," said Jake. I walked toward the farmhouse to see what they'd found. As I approached, I could see them removing bodies, one after the other. The coroner's van was coming up the driveway. The officer waved for the driver to come up beside the farmhouse. "We have several more bodies for you," said one of the officers. "How many do you think you have this time?" said the driver of the van.

"So far, we have discovered six, but we believe there are more. We found several items that might belong to these ladies. There are a couple of bags that contained purses and wallets. We even found shoes and clothing," said the officer. "We are collecting all the evidence and trying to find out who is responsible for doing this and why. Body after body got loaded in the van."

"I need to call for another van to come," said the driver. "We are full.

"The van is on the way and should be here in half an hour," he said as he was leaving.

"Thank you," said the officer.

The day was not starting out as I'd thought it would. This beautiful sunny day was now a crime scene that hadn't ended. After about an hour, the second van had arrived, they pulled out four more bodies. "So far, that is a total of nineteen bodies since yesterday," said the officer.

"Let's hope that is all of them," I said as I walked away. I could see Officer Burns headed in my direction.

"Fancy meeting you here," he smiled at me.

I said, "Well, I thought I would just come and see if they were all finished here.

"They are now up to nineteen bodies," I said. "They found ten more under the farmhouse in a cellar."

One of the officers came over to speak to Officer Burns. "We found ten more bodies and there are no more in the cellar," said the officer.

"Well, I'm glad to hear that," said Officer Burns. "You guys did a great job here."

"We covered the entire area and are convinced there are no more bodies here."

After a few hours, everything was packed up and the officers were leaving. All the evidence was collected and brought back to be examined. "Well," said Officer Burns, "it's time to head back to the station and figure this mess out."

I said, "Yes, let's hope these girls and their families get closure."

I left and headed toward the highway. The day was still nice and sunny, so I headed down a dirt road on the way back. I got out of my car and walked around thinking about the last couple of days. These girls and what they must have gone through. How could someone be so cruel and take lives, I thought? I noticed some blueberry patches, so I grabbed a baggie from my car, and started picking them. I picked a large bag of berries to take home.

I got to the highway and headed toward the cabin. It was time to get home and enjoy the rest of my day. I sat outside on my deck for a few hours to enjoy the sunshine. I went in to watch the news. "A gruesome discovery was found on a property surrounding a farmhouse," said the news broadcaster. "Police have discovered a total of nineteen bodies on the property. There is no information on how long these bodies were on the property. Police will continue their investigation on this discovery."

After about a week, Officer Burns called. "I'm sorry I haven't called sooner, but this case is top priority, and we are trying to get to the bottom of it. We have a few leads about who was living there, and we are now trying to locate them. We believe these bodies have been at the farmhouse for well over twenty-five years. Trying to find out who did this is like a needle in a haystack.

"The reason I called," said Officer Burns, "is, I am wondering if we could meet tomorrow. We are still working on another case and need you to go undercover. My officers here can finish up with the farmhouse case. We are just waiting on results from the evidence that was collected."

I said, "I can be there tomorrow around 9 a.m."

"I will see you then," said Officer Burns.

I woke up to the bright sun shining through my open window. It was a beautiful day with the sound of the birds chirping. I made a coffee and headed out on the deck to enjoy the day. Well, at least a bit of the morning. I had to get ready to go to the police station to meet Officer Burns. After about an hour, I went inside to get dressed and headed into town. I was sure this was the day I had been waiting for. To finally work on a real case with Officer Burns and his team.

I headed down the highway on this nice, sunny, hot day. The traffic was steady but flowing nicely. I have my windows down and the music on. I arrived at the station just before 9 a.m. to meet with Officer Burns. I went inside and made my way down the hall to his office. He was sitting at his desk when I arrived. "Good morning, he said, as he got up from his desk." "Good morning to you too," I said. Let's head down to the conference room so we can talk. "Sandy will be joining us in a few minutes," said Officer Burns. I followed him to the conference room, noticing several pictures on the walls in the hallway. The pictures are of police officers who had retired over the years and a few that were deceased as well.

We entered the conference room and took a seat. "Coffee?" said Officer Burns.

"I would like one," I said. He poured our coffee and we sat down. We both sipped our coffee and waited for Sandy to join us. A few minutes later, Sandy walked through the door. "Good morning. Sorry I'm late," she said with a smile. "I have been working on the case from the farmhouse and trying to find missing women from twenty-plus years ago."

"It's going to take time to get to the bottom of that case," said Officer Burns. I have every available team member working the case. We need to concentrate on the current case we are working on, and let them continue the farmhouse case."

"This is where you come in, Jill," said Sandy. "We need to go over the entire case we are working, so you can get familiar with what we are doing," said Officer Burns. For the past three months, we have been working to find the people responsible for teenage drug and prostitution ring. There are many teenage girls walking the streets and being approached by individuals who are offering them housing and food. The girls are then forced into drugs and prostitution. There is no way out for these girls unless we can put a stop to it. These girls are forced into prostitution or beaten if they don't comply. They are being moved from house to house so they can't be tracked as easy. We have had undercover police working around the clock to keep track of their moves. So far, we found at least four homes they move the girls to. There seem to be at least eight men in and out of the homes and two females who are also working with them. The schedule is for the girls to be loaded in a van and dropped off in different spots downtown. There is always a car watching their every move, so it's hard to get close to them.

Jill, we need to try to get close to one of the ladies, so you can get inside for a better picture of what they are doing. We need pictures and names of some of these girls and leaders. It's not going to be easy, but we have a plan. One of the ladies owns a shop downtown. She watches for homeless girls and offers them help. Once she gets them to trust her, she has them hooked on drugs and on the streets. We need her to trust you and become her new friend.

"I am ready to take this on," I said with a smile. "When do I start?"

"Well, said Officer Burns. "We will get you prepped and ready to start in a few days. We will need to go over everything, from where you lived to your new name. You need to memorize everything because they will drill you. You will need to earn her trust first before she will help you."

"She will have to believe you are also homeless and need her help," said Sandy. "This may take weeks for you to get her to trust you."

"I am ready to do this and whatever it takes," I said.

"OK," said Officer Burns. "We will get you back here tomorrow at 9 a.m., sharp, and start the prep for the case."

"We will see you in the morning," said Sandy.

I got up and said, "Thank you both," and walked away. I went out to my car and felt great about finally starting to work on a real case. This is what I have been waiting for a long time. I drove through town and made my way home to the cabin. It is a nice sunny day, and I didn't want to miss being outside enjoying it. I drove on the quiet highway until I reached my driveway. I went inside and made a coffee. I brought out my music to listen to while I sat in the sun. After about an hour, I got my runners on and went for a walk down the road. It is quiet here and not a lot of traffic. I walked for over 2 kilometres and turned around and headed back home. The horses were in the fields and so peaceful to watch as I made my way back to the cabin.

**I DID GET TO** rake my yard and burn garbage while I was at home. There is always so much to do and so little time to get it done. Today was the day to stay home and get things done that I have been putting off for so long. It felt good to accomplish something and see the result. I have a nice clean yard, and everything is organized and put away. I walked over to where I planted flowers, and nothing grew. Well, I never did have a green thumb. I guess I should have paid attention to when my mom planted flowers. Oh, well, I had fun trying.

I went in to get chicken to cook on the BBQ. The smell of the BBQ just makes me so hungry. I enjoy cooking and eating outside in the sun. After supper, I went for another walk. This time, a shorter walk than earlier. I needed to walk off the big supper I had. At about 10 p.m. I climbed in bed. It is hot in the cabin, so I got up and opened both windows to get a breeze.

I woke at 7 a.m. to the sound of the birds chirping. What a wonderful sound to wake up to. I made a coffee and went outside on the deck to enjoy it. I went back in at 7:45 to get ready to go to the station to prep for the case I will be working on. I am so excited for this day. I left my house at 8:20 so I could go through town and grab a coffee to take with me.

The traffic was light this morning, so I made good time getting to town. I went through the drive-through and got a coffee. I arrived at the station at 8:50. As I got out of my car, I saw Sandy walking towards the door." Hello Sandy," I said with a smile. Hello to you too. "Are you ready for today?" said Sandy. I said, "I am more than ready. "I have been waiting for this day for a long time and it is finally here, "I said with a big smile. "That's good" Sandy said as we walked through the station doors. "Come with me and we will go to the conference room," said Sandy. We both walked down the hall and into the room. "Take a seat and I will be back after I find Officer Burns," said Sandy.

I sat and drank my coffee and waited for them to join me in the room. I sat at a large table with seats for twelve people. The room had a coffee machine in the corner. There was a projector on a table and a screen hanging from the ceiling that could be pulled down. The chairs were big, black, comfy chairs with armrests. After about ten minutes, Officer Burns and Sandy entered the room. "Good morning," said Officer Burns. "Are you ready to get started on the case?"

I said, "Good morning and, yes, I am more than ready."

Officer Burns put a stack of files down on the table as he took a seat across from me. "These are the files on the case and information connected to it. We have dozens of names and places in these files. We are hoping to go through some of this to get you familiar with the case. We have several pictures of the men and women we believe are responsible for this case. We need more evidence before we can go in and make any arrests. We want to take the entire drug/prostitution ring down. If we go in and make a few arrests, they will move the girls somewhere else, and we may never find them. With us, it's having to be all or none in this case."

We looked through some pictures and names of the people involved with taking the girls off the streets. Officer Burns pointed to a picture of a guy named Nick, or better known as Stitch as his street name. We believe he is the ringleader, or at least one of them. He usually stays behind in the houses and has also been seen moving the girls from house to house. This is their way of less traffic coming and going at one place. Less traffic, less nosey neighbours," said Officer Burns. We spent several hours combing through the files and going over pictures.

"It's 12:30 and we should take a lunch break," said Sandy.

"Good idea," said Officer Burns, with a smile. "Let's meet back here at two and finish up at five for the day. Does that sound good to you girls?"

"That's fine by me," I said.

Sandy stood up and said, "See you both back here at two."

All 3 of us left the room and headed down the hall. Sandy and Officer Burns headed in a different direction. They must be going to their officers I thought as I went outside to my car. It is a nice day with a soft breeze blowing. I went to get some food downtown and decided to sit outside in the park to enjoy the beautiful day. I love the sunshine and being outside. The kids were playing in the park and the dogs were running around. I can hear soft cries as a couple of kids collided down the slide. After a few minutes, they are playing again and going up and down the slide.

The time has passed so fast and it's now time to head back to the station. It's already almost 2:00. I headed back to the station which was only 2 minutes away. I parked my car and went inside and made my way to the conference room. Officer Burns and Sandy were at the table when I arrived. "How was your lunch?" asked Sandy.

"It was great," I said with a smile. "I sat in the park and took in the sunshine."

"Well," said Officer Burns. "Let's get back at it. "

We went over and over the files learning more and more about these people. Before we knew it, it was almost 5:00. "This has been a productive day," said Officer Burns." Let's finish for the day and meet back here tomorrow at 9 a.m. he said," as he got up from the table and stretched. "Great, I said, see you tomorrow as I got up and walked out the door and headed to my car."

I headed to the grocery store to pick up a few things I needed. I got home and put my groceries away. I grabbed a cold beer and went out on the deck. I needed a few minutes to unwind and relax before I start supper. My day went well, and this undercover case is very interesting. I am excited to be a part of the team. I started the BBQ and cooked chicken and a bake potatoe. It was delicious and filling. I was now tired after eating the big meal. I sat outside until about 8 p.m. before I headed in the house for the night. I grabbed all the dishes and brought them in the house to wash up. I put leftovers in the fridge for supper tomorrow. At about 11 p.m., it was time to go to bed. I opened the window and climbed into bed for the night.

After several hours of tossing and turning, I decided to get up and sit on the deck. The sky was so bright, and the stars were gleaming. I couldn't get to sleep, so I thought the fresh air would help. I went back inside an hour later and tried again to sleep. I'm not sure if it is all the excitement of this case of just the hot weather keeping me awake. Nevertheless, I needed sleep.

I got out of bed at 6 a.m. after sleeping a total of about three hours. I didn't feel tired, but I knew I would by the afternoon. I got ready and sat out on the deck with my coffee. I wanted to enjoy an hour before I head to work. I packed a lunch to take with me. I enjoyed sitting in the park yesterday and wanted to go back today. I love to sit outside and enjoy the nice weather.

I left the cabin at 8:15, to head to the station to meet Sandy and Officer Burns. I arrived early, so I went inside to the conference room. The door was open, but nobody was there, so I took a seat. I drank my coffee and relaxed until Sandy and Officer Burns walked through the door. "Good morning, "they both said. "Are you ready to start again?" Officer Burns said with a smile.

"I sure am, "I said.

"Well, let's get at it," he said.

We went over more files and looked at several pictures of the suspects. Here is the picture of the lady we believe is responsible for corrupting the girls. She looks for their weaknesses and offers them help. She preys on the young homeless girls. She knows they need help, and she is there to offer it. The only thing they don't know, is they will be owned when they take the help. They are forced into drugs and prostitution before they can blink an eye. They are taught at the very beginning, there is no way out for them. Officer Burns continued explaining the way things work and going over the case.

"We need to end this, and we need to do it fast," said Officer Burns. "These girls are in great danger and have no way out." We went over and over the case for hours. It was lunch time, so we took a break. "I will see you girls back here at 2 p.m.," said Officer Burns. We got up to leave and Sandy went over to open the windows to let a breeze blow through while we were gone. "It's stuffy in here," said Sandy. "Maybe this will help."

We left and headed out for lunch. I went to the park and sat at a picnic table and ate my lunch. It was hot so I didn't have much of an appetite for food. I ate some fruit and drank a bottle of water I had in my cooler. The kids were playing and running around. It felt good to just sit and relax and listen to all the young kids having fun. It is time to go back to the station and finish up for the day.

We met back in the conference room to go over the case again. After a few more hours of prepping, Officer Burns felt confidant I was ready to start my undercover assignment. "OK, Jill," he said with a smile. "We will get you ready tomorrow and start you the next day. Tomorrow will be your final prep day. We will go over everything you will need to do and everything you will need to look for. I will see you ladies tomorrow at 9 a.m., sharp."

**WE LEFT AND I** headed out the door to get to my car. I just wanted to get home and relax on this beautiful sunny day. I won't have many days left to enjoy when I start on this assignment. I headed on the highway towards the cabin. It was such a beautiful day, I decided not to go home. I drove pass my turn and headed in another direction. I wanted to take in some sites before I called it a night. There wasn't much traffic on the highway, so I took my time. The windows were down, and the music is loud. I saw a dirt road to the left just up ahead. It had two big wheels at the entrance. The large gate was open, so I made my way down the long dirt road. I didn't notice any signs of 'Do Not Enter" as I went through the gate. Every once in a while, I will see a private property sign, so I usually just head in and hope nobody lives there. If I notice any movement of living, then I turn around and head in the other direction.

I drove for another five minutes then came across a little water-fall. It looked like it had been there for many years. I stopped and captured a few nice pictures of it and the beautiful scenery. The wildflowers were in bloom and smelt amazing. I walked to the little waterfall to get a few better pictures. There was a little stream and a nice place to get out and walk. I walked along this stream until it ended. I didn't want to take the chance of going any further. It is such a peaceful place to take in. I saw an old boat washed up on the side of the shore and a few indications that people had been there. I snapped a few more pictures and kept walking. There was a fire pit with garbage and smashed bottles around the area. I turned around and headed toward my car. I walked along the water for another fifteen minutes until I could see where I parked my car. It was time to head back home and get some supper.

I drove down the highway until I got to my turn for the cabin. It is a nice day and a great way to end it. I went inside and made supper and went out on the deck to eat. The birds are chirping, and the traffic is still going up and down the highway. I sat outside until about 8 p.m. I went in and watched the news until I went to bed at 11:00. I knew it was going to be a busy day tomorrow getting ready for work.

I woke at 6 a.m. after having a great restful sleep. I made a coffee and went out on the deck. It was quiet and the sun was coming out. I went inside to make my lunch and get ready for work. I left the cabin and headed to the station. I got inside the station at 8:45 and made my way to the conference room to meet Sandy and officer Burns.

A few minutes later, Officer Burns and Sandy walked in the room. We talked for about an hour about the case. "Let's head down to another room where another officer is going to get you all set up for the case." We left and I followed them down the hall until we came to another room. "This is Officer Hall, and she will help get you ready for your assignment. Sandy and I will be back in about half an hour to see how things are going."

"I am Jill," I said with a smile. "Pleased to meet you, Jill. Please call me Sam. I will be getting you ready to go in the field today."

"That's great," I said with a smile.

We went over the clothes they wanted me to wear and how to look like I didn't have much. I had to look like I needed help and had nowhere to live. I needed to earn their trust. I had a few choices of what I could wear, so I chose carefully. I wanted comfortable clothing and shoes. It seemed like I would be doing a lot of walking. I knew it was going to be hot, so I chose a pair of leggings and a tank top. I took a hoody that I could tie around my waist.

"Here," said Sam, "try this hat on and put your hair in a ponytail and through the hole in the back." I put the hat on, and she said it looked great.

"It will keep the sun out of your eyes while you are walking," said Sam. "Here is a pair of cheap sunglasses." She handed them to me. "We don't want you to look like you have too much, so we compromise and give you cheaper items to wear.

"Go change into the items you chose, and I will be right back," said Sam. I went into the bathroom to get dressed into my outfit. I tied my hair up in a ponytail and put on the hat. I changed from my sandals into my runners." OK," said Sam, "let's finish you up. Oh, you look great by the way." She bent down and rubbed a dirty rag on my shoes. "We can't have you out there with a brand-new pair of shoes," she said. She got them looking grubby and put a few pen marks on my hat. She even drew a little heart on the side of my hat and coloured it red. "Let's tie your hoody around your waist and put some bead bracelets on your wrist," Sam said. We were just about done when Officer Burns and Sandy walked in.

"Wow, said Sandy. "You look great."

"Good job, Sam," said Officer Burns. "You sure clean up well— or should I say grubby." I was all ready for the assignment. "One more thing," said Officer Burns. Here is your burner phone. It can't be traced, and it's always tracked to us. We have a van parked near the store where you will be entering. The store is always under surveillance for your protection. We have a camera to attach to your hat. It's a little pin, so we can see your every move. It has video and sound so we can hear everything that is said."

"Well, it looks like you are ready to go," said Sam. "I wish you the best of luck out there and be safe."

I said, "Thank you for all your help," and left the room with Officer Burns and Sandy. We walk outside to the unmarked police car.

"Here is your handgun," said Officer Burns. "You will not be needing it at this time, so we recommend you leave it with us for now. It's the one we had you practise with on the gun course. You should have everything you need to get started. We wish you luck. Now let's go catch the bad guys."

I said, "Let's do this."

We left and drove downtown to where the store is. Officer Burns slowed down and pointed to the store. This is the store the lady in charge works at. "This is where we want you to go and make a new friend," Officer Burns said with a slight smirk. We drove 2 blocks away where the police undercover van with surveillance is parked. Remember, we can hear everything that is said. "If you get into trouble, and need us to move in, you need to say, "I love a good steak", said Officer Burns. "Wow, I said with a smile, how did you come up with that one?" "Well, because I love a good steak," said Officer Burns.

We went inside the van so I could have a look at the system that have. It's neat how it's all set up like this I said with a smile. "Well, said Officer Burns, we need to make sure everyone is safe, and nobody gets hurt." Every once and a while, Sandy will approach the store in her street clothes. She will enter the store and look around and sometimes make a purchase. So don't be alarmed if you see her in the store, especially because you aren't supposed to know anyone in town.

We finished up in the van and I headed down the street to the store. I walk slow and looked around the area to make sure I wasn't being followed. It was a beautiful day and I felt I dressed a little too warm. I usually wear sandals, but not today. I am in my runners and leggings. I pass a coffee shop and a few clothing stores along the way. I finally got to the store. "Well, I said to myself, this is it." It's time to get to work. As Officer Burns says," Let's go catch the bad guys. "

I entered the store and looked around. I could see a lady standing behind the counter. There are 2 other ladies looking around in the store. There is also a lady at the front making a purchase. After the lady paid for her items, she left the store. The lady behind the counter approached me." Can I help you with anything", she said in a soft voice? "No, thank you," "I said. I just came in the store because I felt like I was being followed, "I said with a scared look on my face. "I hope that is O.K, "I said? I didn't know what else to do. "Oh, that's fine the lady said. "Did you happen to get a look at them, "she asked? Well, there was a tall guy with a dark shirt and every time I turned around, I saw him. I got scared, so I came in the first store I saw. The lady went to the door and looked outside to see if she could see him." I don't see anyone out there with that description," she said. "Oh, good, maybe he left" I said.

"Well, my name is Monica," she said with a smile. "Hi, Monica, I said, my name is Beth. "I am new to town, so this is scary for me. "Oh, I understand," said Monica. "Where are you from?" "I am from Toronto," I said with a slight grin. "Oh, what brings you to town?" said Monica. Well, I left a bad relationship and wanted a new start. "What did you do in Toronto?" said Monica. "Well, I rather not go into details, as I am not proud of what I was doing," I said, with my head down. "Well, if you ever need to talk, I am here," said Monica. "Thank you," I said. "It was nice chatting with you, but I must go find a place to get a coffee. "Oh, well if you walk 4 doors down, you will see a nice coffee shop called Mike's Diner," said Monica. They have the best coffee in town and the best food. "It's quiet and you can sit there for hours, and nobody will bother you," Monica said with a smile. "Oh, that's great," I said. "I will head there now, thank you for your help" I said. "Anytime," Monica said.

I left and head to the coffee shop. I want to go there in case Monica is watching me. I am hoping she will show up at lunch time and maybe join me for coffee. I got inside the small but bright little diner. What a cute little place and the atmosphere looks relaxing. I went in and a nice little lady told me to sit anywhere I like. I took a seat in a booth. The waitress came over and asked if I would like a coffee." "I would love a coffee," I said with a smile. She came with my coffee and said, "here is a menu if you would like to look."" Our special today is hot hamburger sandwich with fries or mashed, for $12.95 and includes your coffee," she said with a smile. I said, "thank you," and she walked away. I sat there for about five minutes, and the waitress came back to take my order.

"Just fries," I said.

"Did you want a side of gravy?" she asked.

"No, thank you," I said. "Just the fries."

She took the menu and walked away to put my order in. After a few minutes, she returned with my fries. She set them in front of me with a fork on a napkin. "Enjoy your fries," she said.

"Thank you," I said as I was looking up at her.

I sat and ate my fries. I have been there for over an hour and had three cups of coffee. I decided to get up and go pay for my fries and coffee. I went to the till to pay. "That will be $7.45 "the cashier said with a smile. "Here is ten dollars. Can you give the waitress the change, please?" I will do that; she said and have a nice day."" Same to you" I said as I walked away and headed for the door. I left the diner and walked down the street. My phone rang, so I stopped to answer it." Hello, said officer Burns, can you make your way to the van?"

"I am on my way," I said.

I walk and make sure not to be followed. I go inside the van and shut the door. "Well, that was a great way to start your day," he said.

"I think it did go well," I said." Let's hope you have a new friend," officer Burns said. "We know the lady who calls herself Monica, hangs out at that coffee shop quite often," said Officer Burns. So, I'm sure you will see her there from time to time." Well, I hope so, "I said. I will continue to go there until she shows up. Maybe she will sit with me, and we can talk. "We will have a couple of under-cover officers working the night shift tonight if you are interested in observing," said Officer Burns. You will see the girls being dropped off and working the streets. We need to put together as much information as we can. We need to take them down, but we must have everything in place. "If this is something you would like to be a part of, just let me know," said Officer Burns.

"I would love to come back and see how this is done," I said with a slight tilt of the head. I will head home for a couple of hours and come back around 8 p.m. if that works for you? "That would be fine," said Officer Burns. "Well, it's only 2 p.m. now, so you should go for a walk around and see if you can get familiar with the area," said Officer Burns. "Every once and a while, you will see one of the girls going in the store where Monica works. We believe they fill in from time to time."

Sandy said, "There are only a couple of girls that have ever worked in the store. We believe there is only a couple that can be trusted, so that's why they are chosen to work for Monica."

"I will keep that in mind when I am in the store," I said. "OK, I am off to walk the streets and see what trouble I can get myself into," I said as I opened the door of the van.

I headed up and down the street and walked and walked for a few hours. I was across the street when I noticed Monica heading to the coffee shop. I didn't want to look suspicious and be there at the same time, so I casually walked across the street. I was looking in storefront windows, just browsing. I sat on a bench and drank a coffee I had just bought at a local coffee shop. It was a beautiful day to sit and relax. After about ten minutes, Monica came out of the coffee shop with a bag in her hand. She noticed me and stopped to say hi.

"How are you doing?" she said with a smile.

"I am fine," I said. "Just sitting enjoying the day. What about you? How are you doing?"

"I am doing good," Monica said. "Just picked up food and now heading back to the store."

"Oh," I said, "that's nice. What time does the store close?"

"Oh, well, I close at 7 p.m., six days a week. I take Sundays off for a rest day."

"Everyone needs a rest day," I said. "When I lived in Toronto, I don't think I had too many rest days, so it's nice to have a break from it all."

"That's true," said Monica. "We all need a break. Well, I must get back to the store. Drop by anytime. I would love to chat again."

"I will do that," I said. "Have a great day."

Monica headed back to the store. I sat on the bench a little longer before making my way back to the van. "I will head home now and come back in for tonight," I said.

"That will be great," said Officer Burns.

Sandy said, "I will be here when you get back."

"That's good, see you later," I said. "Oh, I guess I will need a ride back to the station to get my car."

"Oh, right," said Officer Burns with a laugh.

"I will take her," said Sandy. "Just give me a minute and I will be done here," she said with a smile. "Anything to get away from these crazy guy."

We left and headed back to the station. "The sun is still out, and it is such a warm day. So, how was your first day?" said Sandy. "Was it all you thought it was going to be?"

I said, "It was even better. I really enjoy it and look forward to many more like this."

"That's great," said Sandy. "It can get a little intense, so watch your six."

"Always," I said. Well, the traffic was not so bad today.

"Here we are, and I guess I will see you back at the van tonight," said Sandy.

"Yes," I said. "I will see you later and thanks for the ride."

"Anytime," said Sandy. "Oh, when you come back, just park your car around the corner and walk to the van."

"I will and I will be careful," I said.

**I WENT TO MY** car and headed home. I was hungry so I wanted to get something to eat and relax a little before I headed back to work. I sat on the deck with my food and bottle of cold water. It was such a nice day and I wanted to get some relaxing time to myself. I ate and listened to the sounds of the birds and the traffic on the highway. It was so peaceful to just sit and listen to all the different sounds. I sat and went over my day in my head. What a nice day I'd had, and I felt like I'd made a difference today. I met a new friend who, one day, would be my enemy. I couldn't help but think about the girls going through what they were going through each and every day. How Monica thought this was right. Well, maybe she didn't think it was right; maybe the way she was raised or found herself on the streets as well. Sometimes we think there is no way out, so we just do what we are told. For Monica, it was probably her way of surviving now. For whatever reason, we needed to put a stop to this and get those girls off the streets before they were killed.

I spent some time sitting outside and now it was time to go in and get ready to head back to town. This would be my first stakeout and I was excited to see what happened tonight. I did my dishes and got ready to go. I locked my door and made my way to my dirty car sitting in the driveway. I just hadn't had time to wash it, but hopefully on the weekend.

After about a half-hour drive, taking my time and listening to my music, I was on the street over from the police van. I parked and made sure there was nobody around as I got out of my car. I walked around the corner and knocked on the back door to the van. I did message Sandy to tell her I was almost there so she could open the door. She greeted me at the door and said, "Come in and have a look. It's almost 8 p.m. and the girls will be dropped off soon. They will stand at two different corners and wait for cars to pull up. They get dropped off in a white van by two guys.

"Well," said Sandy, "here is the van approaching now." The van stopped, and three young teenage girls dressed in short skirts got out and walked a few feet to the corner. They had a small handbag and high-heeled shoes on. One girl looked so scared, I thought. The van left and went to the other corner a few metres away. Two more girls get out wearing short skirts and high heels. They both went to the corner where it was all lit up. They stood by a fire hydrant and waited for vehicles to pull up. We watched this for over an hour and noticed three girls get into different vehicles. The van that dropped them off was sitting across the road, watching them. "There isn't much we can do at this time until we have everyone in the group to be arrested. We need to take the whole operation down at once," said Officer Burns.

"This just makes me sick," I said.

"Well, this is where we need you to get into these houses so we can get more evidence to make arrests," said Sandy. "We must take them all down and get these girls off the streets. We can't help the life they chose, but for these girls, there is never a way out. They can run, but they are usually found and killed or beaten if they try to get way. These girls have no life, and we need to stop this. After sitting in the van and watching for hours, it is now 1 a.m. These girls have been in so many different vehicles throughout the night."

"I just wanted to get out and grabbed them," I said to Sandy.

"We all do," she said.

"Well", said Officer Burns, "I think you get the full picture now, don't you?"

"I sure do," I said. "This is just sickening."

"Well," he said, "you can make your way to your car and head home. I would like you back here at 9 a.m. tomorrow, and stay close to the store where Monica is. We need you to get her to trust you and get you in with her. Hopefully, she will ask you if you have a place to stay and then offer you a room."

"I am sure it's not going to be that easy, but if she can earn your trust, it should work in our favour," said Sandy. "Well, you guys, have a good night, and I will be back tomorrow."

I left and headed to my car parked around the corner. The streets were quiet, so I got there without a problem. I got in my car and headed around the corner. I could see a couple of girls standing on another corner that were not the girls who got out of the van. I was a little confused as to who these girls were. Did they get dropped off by someone else, or did we miss them getting dropped off first? I parked and waited to see what was going to happen and if the girls were going to be picked up by anyone. After about thirty minutes, a car pulled up and approached the girls. They were wearing tight pants and high-heel shoes. A black car pulled up and the girls went over to the passenger-side window. I could see the driver wearing a baseball cap and he leaned over to talk to the girls. The one girl put her head in the window to talk to him. After a minute, she opened the door and got in. The other girl stayed back and went on the sidewalk and stood against the window of a store. I wrote the make and model of the car and a partial plate as he drove away. I had no idea who these girls were or if it was the same pimps who pimped them out. All I could do was keep the info and pass it onto Officer Burns tomorrow when I came back to work.

It was now almost 2 a.m., and time to head home. The drive home was quiet and there was not much traffic. I rolled my window down and let the cool breeze blow through. I needed to stay awake as I was getting so tired. I turned off the highway and made it to the cabin. I was never so happy to see my little place in the woods. I went inside and got ready for bed. I watched a few minutes of TV, and then crawled into bed. I got up after a few minutes and opened both windows to let the breeze blow through. I fell asleep fast and woke at 6 a.m. I knew that was not much sleep, but for me, it was. I made a coffee and went outside to enjoy the sun. It was going to be a nice day.

I stayed out on the deck until 7:30, and then went in to get ready for work. At 8:15, Officer Burns called and told me not to come in until eleven. "You had a late night he said, so stay home and enjoy the sun and we will see you at eleven."

I said "OK," and hung up the phone. *Well, that's a good start to my day*, I thought. *I will sit outside a little longer and take in the sun. The birds are chirping, and the traffic is moving fast up and down the highway. I am still tired, so this is just the medicine I need right now.* I made some toast and went back out on the deck. My fire pit was full of ashes and my yard needed to be raked. Oh, well, I would get to it on the weekend, I hoped. My job was important so that took priority over anything right now. I went inside to get ready to go to town. I was going to stop by the store to see Monica and ask her how things were going.

I got to town at 10:45 and parked my car on the other street around the corner. I called Officer Burns to let him know I was in to start my shift. He said, "Good luck and let's get this done safely."

"I will," I said.

We hung up and I walked down the road. I sat on the bench outside the store where Monica worked. I thought I would sit there and see if she came out. I sat for an hour, and I could see her in the corner of my eye, looking out the store window. She knocked on the window and I turned around. She gave me a wave of the hand and I waved back. She smiled and I smiled back. *Well, that's a good start,* I thought to myself. At about 12:30, one of the girls I recognized entered the store. I had seen her there before so she must be one of the girls that fill in once and a while. A few minutes later, Monica came out of the store. "How are you today?" she said with a smile.

I said, "I am fine, and you?"

"I am good," said Monica. "Would you like to join me for a coffee at the coffee shop?"

"I would love to," I said. I got up and we walked down the street to the coffee shop. We went inside and sat in a booth at the back of the shop.

"What a beautiful day out there," I said.

"It sure is. Too bad I must work," said Monica.

"Well, take a few days off and enjoy yourself," I said.

"I wish it was that easy. I really don't have anyone to work the store more than a couple of hours at a time," she said.

"Well, you can always train me, "I said with a smiley grin. "I worked in retail for many years before I switched jobs."

"Well, I will keep that in mind," she said with a smile.

"I will have to work under the table," I said. "I can't have anyone know where I am. I left on bad terms to get out of the life I was living. I was tired of being hit and slapped around. It was good money, but I couldn't take the beatings. Now, I am going to run out of money soon, so I will need a side job of some sort. Just not sure what that will be if I can't go on payroll."

"Well," said Monica, "let me see what I can do." Maybe helping me in the store is not such a bad idea. "Then, you can be trained at the same time so I can take a day off here and there," said Monica. "That sounds good," I said. I would love to help you out. "Where are you staying right now," Monica asked? I am staying in a little Motel down the road. "It's cheap and walking distance to everything I need," I said. We sat and drank coffee for over an hour, losing track of time." Oh, said Monica, I really must get back to the store." My girl is only there for an hour and its passed that now." Oh, an hour "I said. Why don't you keep her longer so you can enjoy your break? I can't, because she had other commitments and I am lucky to get her for an hour at a time. It helps me if I need to run out for bit. "I understand," I said. "Well, I must go, and the coffee is on me, said Monica as she put money on the table."" Well, thank you "I said with a smile. "Stop by anytime," said Monica. We both got up and went to the door.

"Goodbye," said Monica.

"Goodbye to you, too," I said.

**I WENT OUT AND** walked down the street toward the police van. I kept walking past and my phone rang. It was Officer Burns. "Hello," he said. "Well, that went well. Looks like you might have a job soon. It seems like she is starting to trust you, but just be careful. It could be a test, so watch your back. We will need to get you a room at the motel down the street. We wouldn't want Monica checking up on you now, would we?"

"No, I guess not," I said with a smile. "I didn't want to tell her I was homeless, so I had to say something. I did tell her I had to make cash though."

"Yes, we heard everything," said Sandy. "You did a good job, and it sounds like she is trusting you."

"Yes, I believe she is," I said. "Can I stop by the van to talk for a few minutes? I have something I need to tell you about last night."

"Sure, come by and come in the back door. Just be careful nobody sees you," said Officer Burns.

I carefully walked to the back of the police van and climbed inside. "I was on my way home last night when I went to my car and noticed a couple of young ladies on the other street corner. I watched them for a little while and they were approached by a driver. I knew they were working the streets but was wondering if it was the same girls owned by the same pimps."

"Well, we know the girls you are talking about," said Officer Burns. "Unfortunately, these ladies are older than you think, and we will only be able to take them in and charge them with prostitution. These ladies have been working that corner for several years and have been charged numerous times. They keep going back so we just leave it at that and concentrate on the younger girls right now. The young teens are our priority and are the ones who need our help."

"I understand that fully, "I said. "I wasn't aware there were others around the corner."

"Oh, there are many corners if you look hard enough," said Sandy.

"Well, I better get back out there and look like I need help living on the streets," I said with a smile.

I left the police surveillance van and made my way to the bench in front of the store where Monica worked. I was sitting having a coffee when I realized it was almost time for supper. I wasn't sure what time I was heading home that night. I left the bench and went to the coffee shop to get a takeout chicken burger and fries. I went back to sit and eat on the bench. Monica came outside and sat beside me. She said, "the store is empty so I thought I would come visit."

"Well, that is nice of you," I said with a smile. "How had your day been?"

"My day is fine. The store was super busy today. So many people looking for sandals and sunglasses. I am glad I have a lot of stock to keep everyone happy."

"Well, that's good," I said. "Hopefully I can afford a pair of sandals soon. I need to be careful with my spending. Having a roof over my head and to be able to eat is my priority right now."

"That makes sense," said Monica. "I understand where you are coming from like it was yesterday. I have been on the streets before and wouldn't wish it on anyone. I try to help anyone I can, if possible."

"Well, that's the feeling I get when we talk," I said to Monica. "We need more people like you out there."

"Well, thank you," she said with a huge smile. "I need to go back in the store and get ready to close. I am going to close early today and give myself a break. It's not much of a break, but an hour is better than nothing."

"You got that right," I said.

"Well, thanks for the chat and maybe we can have coffee again tomorrow," Monica said as she got up off the bench."

"I'm sure I can fit that into my busy schedule," I said as she walked away. I could hear her laughing as she walked into the store.

The cars were driving by, and the buses were stopping at the bus stops. People were on and off the buses and heading home for the night. The stores were closing, and the streets were busy. I stayed sitting on the bench until Monica came out of the store and locked the door behind her. "Good night, Beth," she said as she walked away.

"See you tomorrow," I said as she headed to her car. I waited a few minutes, and then made my way to my car. I knew it was time to call it a night. I called Officer Burns when I got in my car. "I am done for the night and heading home if that's OK," I said.

"Yes, you can make your way home and we will see you tomorrow."

I left and headed home to the cabin. I was tired and needed to sit out and get some more fresh air. The windows were down as I drove the quiet highway home. The breeze was blowing my hair from side to side as I drove home to relax. I could smell the fires and noticed smoke in the air. This was a bad time of year for fires because of the extreme heat we had been having and no rain to soak the grass. It was nice to live off the grid and have a small fire in my fire pit. I arrived at the cabin and made my way inside. I threw on some comfy clothes and grabbed a cold beer. It was time for me to sit and relax and think about my day. I felt confident that Monica was starting to trust me more and more every day. I just needed her to trust me enough to take me in. I was sure in time it would all work out. I could tell Monica was a caring person for these girls. I was sure deep down, she knew what she was doing was wrong, but to her it was a job. I couldn't wait for the day we took them all down and ended this. It would never be over, but at least it was a start. We took them down one by one.

It was 9:00 and the sun was just starting to set. The stars were out, and the sky was so bright. I loved sitting and watching the stars. Well, it was time to head inside and get something to eat. It had been a productive day and I was back tomorrow. I made a toasted chicken sandwich and a cup of tea. I sat inside to eat while I watched the news. There wasn't much on TV so I called it a night at about 11:30. I opened the windows and let the breeze blow through. I could smell the smoke from the fires burning. It must be the way the wind is blowing I thought. Living in the woods makes you smell so many different things, including the animals.

I woke at 6 a.m. and headed out on the deck with my first cup of coffee. It was going to be a nice day. I didn't want to dress too warmly, walking up and down the streets. I had to go through the clothes I was given to wear while I was working. I didn't have much for summer clothes, so I had to make it work. I wrapped my hoody around my waist, so it was cooler. I left the house and headed into town to hit the streets, as Officer Burns called it.

I drove in and carefully parked a block over and made sure nobody was around when I got out of my car. The streets were quiet, so I headed down toward the store where Monica worked. I went to the coffee shop and picked up a coffee to go. I made my way to the bench and took a seat. I sat beside another lady sitting on the other end.

"It's a nice day today," she said with a smile. I said, "It is and it's going to get hotter."

"Good, she said. "But not too hot. I love the heat, but it can make you sick if it's too hot."

"Yes, you are right, we need to be careful," I said. "Here comes the bus."

"It was nice talking to you, "the little lady said softly.

"Yes, have a great day," I said.

The little lady made her way onto the bus as it stopped with the sound of squeaky brakes. The bus left and headed down the street, stopping at every stop sign. I could hear the squeaky brakes at every stop until it got farther away. The sidewalks were getting busy with people walking and going in store to store. I was waiting for Monica to come out and talk to me. I was hoping we could meet for a coffee at the coffee shop. I waited until about noon, and she still didn't come out. I was getting hungry but wanted to wait for her. At about 12:45, I noticed a young girl going into the store. It was the same girl I'd seen go in the other day. I guessed she was there to give Monica a break. Maybe she would come out soon and go for lunch. I waited for about half an hour, and finally Monica came out of the store. "Hi," she said with a smile. Fancy meeting you here."

I laughed and said, "Not much more to do than sit and relax."

"You got that right," Monica said. "Would you like to join me for lunch?"

"I would love to join you, Monica."

"Great, let's go to the little coffee shop and get some food," she said. "I am starving so I got one of my friends to watch the store for an hour or so."

"Well, that's good," I said. "You need a break from it all."

We walked to the coffee shop making small talk. Monica held the door as we walked inside. We made our way to the back booth and had a seat. The waitress came over to clear the table and give it a good wipe. "I will be right back with the menu," she said with a smile. "Would you ladies like coffee to start?" "Yes," we both said.

The waitress returned a few minutes later with our coffees. "Here is the menu and I will be right back to take your orders," she said. We looked through the menu and decided what to order. "How is the club house, Monica?" I said with a smile.

"It is great, and they use real turkey," she said.

"Good, that's what I am going to have," I said. "But with onion rings and not fries."

"You know, I think I am going to have the same thing today," said Monica.

"That sounds good," I said.

The waitress came back, and we placed our orders. "Two club-house sandwiches with onion rings," Monica said.

"Do either of you want a side of gravy?" she asked.

"Not for me," I said.

"Just ketchup for me," said Monica.

"It will be ready in a few minutes."

"So, Beth," said Monica, "how are you surviving out there?"

"Well," I said, "I have a little bit of savings to get me through until I run out. I really need to pick up a job or some type of work. I made good money before I moved here, so I was able to save."

"It won't last forever," Monica said.

"No, it won't, so I need to find a part-time job to keep me going. I am afraid I will be on the streets before long if I don't find some way to make money.

"Well, if you don't mind me asking, what did you do before you moved here?" said Monica. I looked at Monica with a side grin and said, "I am not proud of the person I am and what I did most of my life. I wouldn't want to be judged I said, so it's best you don't know."

"Oh, Beth, I wouldn't judge you at all. We all have skeletons in the closet."

"I feel shamed at my lifestyle and how I lived for so many years," I told Monica. "I lost my family to a tragic accident and had nowhere to go," I said. "I was fifteen years old and the only way for me to survive was on the streets. I didn't have any money or any place to live. I had no other family to take me in. I went from foster home to foster home until I couldn't take the abuse anymore. I kept running away and they finally gave up on me. Before I knew it, I was homeless. Then I was approached by a lady who helped me survive by taking me in. Well, the rest, you can figure out. It was the only way for me to eat and have a roof over my head. It was that or be killed on the streets. I met a man who was trafficking women and that's how my life went for many years until they had me recruiting young girls. I guess I was getting too old to keep me on the streets so I had to find young blood, as they would say."

"So why did you leave if you were happy there?" said Monica.

"Well, I got involved with one of the pimps and he started getting more abusive every day. So, I had enough of the beatings, and I ran away from him."

"Oh," said Monica, "that makes perfect sense."

"So that is why I can't make money or be put on any payroll. I don't want him to track me."

"Well, I understand," said Monica. "I will try to help you. Let me see what I can do in the next few days, now that I know what experience you have."

"That would be great," I said. "I'm sure my money won't last much more than another month, so I will need to figure something out soon."

We finished eating and Monica had to get back to the store. "I really need to get back and let my friend go home," said Monica. We stood up and went to the counter to pay for our food. We went outside and walked toward the store.

"Well, I guess this is it," said Monica. "I will see you soon."

"I will see you soon," I said, "and have a great day." I sat on the bench while Monica went inside the store. A few minutes later, the young girl came out and got in a van parked across the street. The girl looked well dressed and was wearing a lot of makeup. It was a beautiful sunny day but too hot to be sitting in the sun with pants on. I couldn't find shade, so I went for a walk and stayed close to the storefronts, out of the sun. After about an hour, I sat back down on the bench in front of the store. I could see Monica in the store front window fixing a display. After a few minutes, I could hear someone call me.

"Beth," I heard in a soft voice, "can you come inside and help me move something?"

I turned around to notice it was Monica asking me for help. I said, "Sure, I can help you." I got up and went inside the store. "We just need to move this mannequin out of the window so I can undress her and put a different outfit on her," said Monica.

"OK, let me help. You hold the base at the legs, and I will get the top of her." We managed to get her out of the window and put her down on the floor. "Wow," I said, "is this the outfit you are putting on her?" "Yes," said Monica. I just got a few of these in and they are beautiful for this time of year."

"You got that right," I said with a huge smile. "I love the colour and the material is so soft."

"Yes, the material is nice, and light," said Monica.

I started to undress the mannequin while Monica chose jewelry to add to top it off. "How about this?" she said with a smile, as she showed me what she chose.

"That looks amazing," I said. "Do you have a silk scarf?"

"Yes, I do," said Monica. "What colour do you think? "

"I think a soft yellow, but it must be plain to enhance the colour of the outfit," I said.

"Let me go out back and look at what colours I have." Monica came back after a few minutes, holding four different soft, plain-coloured scarves. "Oh, let me look," I said. Those colours are beautiful. "All but this one will look good," I said. But I think we should tie this one around the hair and make it look summery. I chose the soft yellow and tied it around her hair and put a loose bow in the back. "Wow," said Monica. "That looks amazing," she said with a huge smile. Where did you learn to dress a mannequin so well? Many years ago, I worked in a clothing store and my job was dressing mannequins. "Well, you sure have talent," said Monica. Anything else I can help you with today? "I have a few boxes to unpack if you want to help," said Monica. Sure, I can help I said. "It's much cooler in here than sitting out in the sun," I said. Yes, it is." I can only sit a few minutes in the sun," said Monica.

**MONICA TOOK ME OUT** back and showed me the boxes to open. We spent a few hours taking clothes out and hanging them on the racks. Every once and a while, Monica could hear the door of the store open, and she would go deal with the customers. We unpacked about 12 boxes of articles. "We got so much done today," said Monica. You have been a lot of help today, Beth. "Oh, it was my pleasure," I said with a smile. "It kept me busy and out of the sun," I said. I am going to go get a cold drink, would you like me to get you something I asked Monica? "I would love a strawberry milkshake," she said. "The coffee shop has great milkshakes," she said. Perfect, I will go get milkshakes for both of us. Monica went to the till and got out $20. Here, take this money. The milkshakes are my treat for all your help today." Oh, thank you," I said. I took the money and went to the coffee shop to get the milkshakes.

"Well, that was successful," I said. I knew Officer Burns and the crew could hear my every word. I ordered the milkshakes to go and headed back to the store. "Here is yours and here is the change, "I said with a smile. "Thank you so much for this," Monica said. I wouldn't have gotten all this done without your help. "I enjoyed our day together and it kept me out of the sun as well," I said. We chatted for about an hour, and Monica said she had to get ready to close the store. "I think I am going to close an hour early today," she said. It's one of the girls birthdays today and we are having a BBQ for supper. "Oh wow, I said. That sounds like fun." "Well, you have yourself a good evening," I said, as I make my way to the door. "Thanks," said Monica, and I will see you tomorrow.

I left and decided to sit out on the bench. I think I got a brain freeze from drinking the milkshake so fast. It was delicious and worth the brain freeze I thought as I laughed out loud. I could hear the squealing of brakes and people getting on and off buses as I watched from the bench. About a half hour later, Monica came out of the store and locked it behind her. "I will see you tomorrow," she said as she walked away. "Yes, "I said. See you tomorrow and enjoy the birthday. "Thanks, "she said. I waited for Monica to get to her car, and I left and walk down the street to get to my car. I was parked around the corner but had to make sure I wasn't being followed. I am happy the day turned out the way it did. I felt like Monica, and I were becoming friends but still must be careful at the same time. Always have your guard up as I was taught.

I stop at the van before I head home. Officer Burns and Sandy were there. "What a great day today," said Sandy. "That sure went well," said Officer Burns. Yes, I said it went better than I thought." I think I am going to head home, and I will be back tomorrow," I said. "Have a great night," they both said as I left the van. I head home to enjoy the rest of the evening. It is still hot out and I am hungry. I put the windows down and let the breeze blow through as I drove the busy highway home. The traffic started to get slower as I make my way down the highway. I hear an ambulance and I pull over with the rest of the traffic. The ambulance flew by and so did a police car. There must be an accident I thought. I hope nobody was hurt. I drive another 2 or 3 minutes when suddenly, the traffic comes to a complete stop. There is a flag man up ahead, stopping all the traffic from going any further. I stop and shut my car off. I know it was going to be a long wait. It is hot so I had to keep starting my car to keep cool. After about 10 minutes, a tow truck went through to get to the accident. The ambulance heads back to town with the sirens on. This can't be good I thought. It is about half an hour when finally, the traffic started to move. Slow but sure I thought as we crawled forward to get by the accident. I can see a blue car in the ditch. It is upside down and there was articles all over the ground. I got through and made it towards my turn off. I am glad to be home after this hot day.

I go inside to change into something cooler. I am in pants all day and it was so hot. I grab a cold drink and go out on the deck to enjoy the rest of my day. I sit for about an hour, then go inside to get some food. I heat up leftovers and go out on the deck to eat. I am happy today went well with Monica. I think she is really starting to trust me. I just hope she will trust me enough to have me work for her from time to time. At about 7 p.m. I go in to get another cold drink. It is such a beautiful evening out. The sky is well lit up and the birds are singing. I bring out my music to listen to as I sit alone and enjoy the tunes. I stay outside for another couple of hours before I head back inside for the night.

I watch the news for an hour then crawl into my bed. It is hot so I get up and open the windows to let a breeze blow through. I toss and turn until it is morning. I can see the sunlight coming through the windows and knew it is time to get up. Coffee is calling my name. I sit outside for a couple of hours before I get ready for work. I head in around 9 a.m. to start my day. I park on the other street around the corner. I walk to the coffee shop and get a coffee. I was sitting on the bench when Monica comes to open the store. "Good morning," she said, as she walked by and opened the door with the key. "Good morning," I said with a smile. I sit on the bench until about 11 a.m. Monica didn't come out once to see me. I thought maybe she must have been busy doing something. People are in and out of the store. Some are coming out with bags of merchandise.

I left and went to walk down the street to look at the other stores. I didn't want to sit on the bench, day after day and cause any suspicion with Monica. I must make her think I am walking and taking in the sites. I go back to the bench at around 2p.m. Monica is still nowhere to be seen. I didn't see her leave for lunch. At about 5p.m. Monica comes out of the store and locks the door. I turned around and asked her if she was alright. "I am fine," she said. I had a little bit of a mishap last night at the BBQ. One of the girls got a little out of hand. "Oh, no," I said. "Is everything OK?"

"Yes, well it will be," said Monica. "We have a few things to take care of when I get home. A couple of the girls had a little too much to drink and they got into a fight. I had to step in and break it up, but not without a punch to the face first."

"Oh, wow," I said. "That looks sore."

"It looks worse than it is," said Monica.

"I should have come with you to be your bodyguard," I said with a laugh.

"Yes, you should have come to protect me," she said with a slight smile.

"Next time," I said.

"Well, there won't be a next time for a while," said Monica. "My nice days with these girls are over until they can behave and learn to get along together."

"I don't blame you. How many kids do you have?" I asked.

"Well, they are not my kids, just girls that I look after. We all live in one big house, so it gets hard at times."

"I guess it would, but at least you have company and are never alone at night."

"Yes, I guess there are some advantages to this," said Monica.

"Well, I must go now and head home. It has been a crazy day and I have things to deal with when I get home."

"OK," I said. "I will talk to you tomorrow. If you need any help, don't hesitate to ask."

"I may take you up on that soon," said Monica. I sat on the bench for a few more minutes until I knew Monica was gone. I went to my car and left for the night. It had been a long day just sitting around doing nothing. I was bored but it was worth the wait in the end. I got home and got changed into something cooler. I sat on the deck for a little while before making supper. It was still hot, so I just made a salad to eat. I didn't feel like cooking in the heat.

I spent the night relaxing and doing outdoor work for an hour. My yard needed to be raked and the fire pit needed to get emptied. I got both done and then went inside for the night. I got ready for bed and watched a show. I was falling asleep, so I shut the TV off and went to bed. The breeze was blowing through the cabin, and it felt so nice and cool. I had a good sleep and woke at 6 a.m. I made a coffee and took it out on the deck. The birds were singing, and the traffic was up and down the highway.

At 8 a.m., I went inside to get ready for the day. My phone rang and it was Office Burns. "How are you doing?" he said.

"I am fine and things are going good with Monica. She seems to be trusting me and confiding in me," I said.

"Yes, it sure sounds like she is trusting you. Just watch your six and make sure you are careful getting in and out of your car. We don't want her knowing you have a car."

"I understand, and I will be careful. I will be heading in to work in about an hour," I told Officer Burns as I poured my coffee.

"Great, we will see you later when you get to town," he said.

**I FINISHED GETTING READY** and left the cabin to head to work. It sounded like Officer Burns wants to get this case wrapped up sooner than later. I had to try my hardest to get this accomplished. I get to town after driving for over twenty-five minutes. The traffic was heavier this morning than usual. I park on the other street and walk over to the bench in front of the store. I sit for a few minutes and then I walk down the street to get a coffee at the coffee shop. It is busy in there, so I must wait a few minutes. As I stood in line, Monica walked in. "Hello, "she said with a smile." Oh, hi Monica," I said. How was your evening last night? It was good. I got some things worked out with the girls. Man, those teenagers are hard on the head. They think they know everything, and you can't talk to them." Yes, they sure do," I said. Well, I am here if you ever need help talking to them. "Thanks," said Monica. "Are you busy today?" asked Monica. "No, what would I be doing?" I said with a smile. I have all the time in the world. I want to look for a job, but I can't be traced right now. Well, I talked things over with one of my fellow friends and I think it's a good idea if we get you to help me out at the store. It will be only part time right now to see how things work out, but I can really use the help. "That's if you are interested," said Monica.

"That sounds good," I said. "When did you want me to start?"

"Well, how about today?" said Monica. "Does that work for you, or do you need more time to think about it?"

"No, that sounds great," I said with a large smile.

"Wonderful," said Monica. "Come to the store after you get your coffee.

"Great, I will see you shortly," I said.

*Wow*, I thought. *This is the break we need. I just got my foot in the door.* I got my coffee and slowly walked to the store, knowing Monica was behind me after she got her coffee. After a few minutes, she caught up to me.

"Well, let's get going so I can show you how to open the store," said Monica.

"Alright, let's get going," I said. We walked back to the store and opened the door with the key. Monica said, "here is the alarm when you enter the store. You have ten seconds to key in the code before the alarm goes off. This is the code: 1234 and then hit the # sign."

"OK, well, that is easy to remember," I said.

We put the OPEN sign in the window and got the till ready.

"Today, we will get some new stock out," said Monica. "I have eight boxes to unpack and hang up. You will probably have to steam some of the items, but I will show you how."

"Great," I said. "I have done this before, so hopefully I'm not too rusty."

"Well, that's good to know. I will go out and get a couple of boxes for us to unpack. I have some nice outfits I want to see. I ordered them a few weeks ago, and they finally arrived."

"Oh, great," I said with a smile. "Can't wait to see them."

Monica brought two large boxes to the front of the store. "Let's start here," she said. "OK, "I said. I grabbed the utility knife and opened box # 1. Oh, the colours. "Absolutely beautiful," I said as I saw the teal outfit on top.

"Yes, they are supposed to be nice, bright colours. I can't wait to see them," said Monica. We spent the better part of the day unpacking and getting stock hung up and on the racks. Before we knew it, it was 1:00.

"It's one o'clock," said Monica. "Time for some lunch."

"Wow, I was wondering why I felt so hungry," I said to Monica, as I crushed the cardboard boxes.

"What would you like for lunch?" asked Monica.

"I could eat a horse right now," I said. "But I will settle for a clubhouse and fries. That sounds good. I will go to the coffee shop and get some lunch. Are you OK to stay here if I go? "Yes," I said. "I will be fine." I will clean up this mess while you are gone.

Monica left the store and heads to the coffee shop. I wait until I couldn't see her, and I tried to snoop around. I must grab the garbage and get it put back before she arrives with the food. I am trying to hurry but be careful at the same time. I look-in a file cabinet but couldn't see anything useful. I did notice a cabinet with a lock on it. I tried to get it open, and I look for a key in her desk. No luck finding the key and no luck getting it open. Well, I will find another way when I have more time I thought. I must get back out front before she gets back with lunch. I continued cleaning up the mess from the stock, as Monica walked in. "Wow, this looks great and the mannequin in the window, looks amazing with that new outfit," said Monica. "I am so glad you like it," I said with a smile. "You are such a great help today," said Monica. We got so much done. I feel like I wasn't rushed and had fun at the same time. I'm glad." I had a lot of fun as well, "I said.

We spent the remainder of the day sorting and getting a large sale rack ready. "Let's do this at 25 percent off," said Monica. This stuff isn't selling, so we need to make room for more new stock. "Great," I said. "Let's get this done so we can put out new stuff tomorrow and finish all those boxes of stock," I said. I was trying to see if she will want me back tomorrow, so I offered to help again. "Ok," said Monica. Let's get this done.

"It's 5:30, so I think we did enough today to be able to close at six today," said Monica.

"Sure, that works," I said. "I will be back tomorrow if you would like the help."

"Absolutely," said Monica. We both left the store at six and headed home. I let Monica go to her car and after I knew she was gone, I went to the van to see Officer Burns.

"Well, that was great that you got in the store to work," said Officer Burns. "Now we just need her to offer you a place to live."

"Yes," I said. I was thinking I would tell her after next week, that I have no money left and I will be on the streets if I can't find a cheap place to lay my head.

"Great idea, "he said. "You are doing great, and we know now, she trusts you."

I left and headed home. "This was a very productive day, and I felt like I got something accomplished. I knew deep down, Monica trusted me. Well, hey, it's me. What's not to trust?" I laughed out loud. I felt like I was on Cloud Nine as I drove home. I sat outside with a cold beer as I listened to the birds singing. What a great day I thought. I spend the night cleaning the yard and enjoy the weather. I had a good night's sleep, and it was time to get ready to go to town. After sitting outside in the sun for an hour, I went in to get ready to go to work.

I got to town and sat on the bench waiting for Monica to get to the store. At 8:45, she arrived and opened the door. "Come on in," she said with a smile. "I had so much fun yesterday and we accomplished so much work. "Let's see what we can get done today Beth as she went to make a pot of coffee. "Sounds good to me," I said as I put the open sign in the window.

I worked at the store for the next few days, helping as much as I could. I needed to impress Monica and show her how hard

I worked. I arranged stuff around the store and started unpacking the stock as quickly as it came in. Monica was going around the store singing and in such a good mood all day long. "Today is Friday, so I would like to know if you would like to work alone tomorrow? I would love to have a day off and not have to worry about the store. I feel confident that you can do this on your own," she said with a smile.

"I would love to work tomorrow. You really need a day off," I said. "Go and enjoy yourself and don't worry about the store. I got this."

"I told my friend about you, and he said it is good that I finally have a friend I can trust. He would love to meet you if you are willing to come for a barbecue at our house on Sunday."

"That would be nice," I said. "What would you like me to bring?"

"Just yourself. You have already helped me enough. I need to figure out a pay for you."

"Well, you can help me by finding me a place to live," I said. "I am almost out of money and really don't want to sleep on the streets. I did that way too many times. I don't think my body can take it anymore."

"I will see what I can do," said Monica.

After working all day and getting so much done, it was time to lock up and go home. "Here are the keys and this is the code. I wrote it down so when you arrive tomorrow, the alarm doesn't go off."

"Perfect," I said. Thank you and have a good day off and I will see you on Sunday. On the paper was the address for the barbecue. We both walk out together, and she heads to her car. I wait until she is gone and make my way to the police van to see Officer Burns. I bang on the back door and Officer burns opens it. "Come on in," he said with a smile. You sure are doing a great job. "We are so close to making arrests and getting these people off the streets for good," he said. I will be at the store alone tomorrow but need to open the locked cabinet somehow. Is there a way to get in it without breaking the lock? "Yes, "he said. I have a locksmith that can open it for you. He will be there at 11 a.m. tomorrow. "Go through what you can and get pictures if you find anything useful," said Officer burns. We need every bit of evidence possible. "Perfect," I said. "I am going to head home now, and I will be back to open the store at 9 a.m. tomorrow. Well, I will probably be there a bit earlier."

I headed home on the nice, sunny day. I got a cold drink and sat out on the deck. After about an hour, I went in to make supper. I sat out until 8 p.m. to enjoy the singing of the birds. I was sitting back thinking about finally being in the store alone. I had to make sure there were no cameras watching anything that went on inside. I didn't want to get caught snooping around. That would be a disaster. I went to bed at about eleven, and opened the windows for a nice, cool breeze to blow through.

**I WOKE UP EARLY** and couldn't get back to sleep. *Well, it's time to get up and start my day,* I thought. *I can't do it by staying in bed.* I laughed out loud. I guess I just had so much going through my mind and today was a big day for me. I got ready and headed to town to open the store. The traffic was usually slow this time of day, so I took my time and listened to music all the way in. I got to the store and opened the door and shut the alarm off. I waited and it didn't go off. I locked the door behind me because it was too early to open. I went out back and sat at the table to finish my coffee. I casually looked around to make sure I wasn't being watched. I couldn't see anything out of the ordinary. I went out front and opened the store. I turned the open sign around in the window.

It was now almost 11 a.m., and I was expecting someone to come and open the locked cabinet. I hoped this wasn't a waste of time and we found some evidence in there. We really needed to nail these guys fast. Officer Burns called to say Sam was on his way and to expect him shortly. At 11:05, Sam arrived and introduced himself.

"It's back here in the back room," I said as I led the way. He looked at the cabinet and said, "This will be easy." He took out his tools and had the cabinet opened in fewer than twenty seconds. The lock popped open. "Well, I guess that's it," he said with a smile. "You can just put the lock back on it when you are done. Nobody will know it was ever open."

"Thank you," I said. Sam left and I opened the cabinet. There were files after files in there. So many names and, as I went through them, I saw pictures of girls. There were dates and times. Where they are from and when they took them in. I took picture after picture of everything I saw. "I think I hit the jackpot," I said, knowing Officer Burns was listening. I went as fast as I could so I could lock it back up. It took me over a half hour to get everything I needed. I locked the cabinet and went out front. Officer Burns called and said Sandy was coming for my phone. They needed to get everything off it and erase it. We hit the motherlode and that's what we needed.

About an hour later, Sandy showed up. She looked around the store as we talked. I handed her my phone to take back to the police van to download all the pictures. "I will get this back to you soon," Sandy said as she left the store.

"OK," I said. "See you soon."

At about 2:00, Monica called to check in. "How are you doing with the store?" she said. "Is everything going well?"

I said, "Everything is fine. A few busy times but other than that, it's all good. You enjoy your day, and I will see you tomorrow, Monica."

"OK, see you tomorrow."

Sandy comes back with my phone. We got a lot of evidence from the pictures you took. We cleared your phone just in case it gets in the wrong hands. There are girls dating back the last few years. Some of them had an X through their face. Other pictures showed them tied up and beaten. We need you now to work your magic and get her to offer you a place to live. "Hopefully at the BBQ tomorrow," I said. You might want to tell her you will work at the store for payment for living there. I will think of something but that sounds like a great idea if she brings it up. Well, good luck tomorrow. We all know you can get her to talk.

The day finally comes to an end. I set the alarm and lock the door. It was time to head home for the night. I get back to my car and head on the highway. I am tired and need to relax on my deck. My body is not used to working all day. I spent the better part of the evening on the deck. I make a sandwich and couldn't finish it all. I watch a show and go to bed at midnight. I can hear the birds singing as I tried to sleep. My windows are open to let the breeze blow through.

It's Sunday and time to get up and start my day. I did some yard work and then go inside to get ready to go to town. I want to get a dessert to bring with me to the BBQ. I grab a chocolate cake and park my car around the corner from the store. I have to call a cab to go to Monica's house. It's almost 4, so a good time to get there for supper. Then I can offer to help her cook or set the table. I went around the corner to where the cabs park. I tap on the window to see if he was available. He waved for me to get in. "Where to, mam?" he said. I showed him the paper with the address. After about 5 minutes of driving, the cab driver stops the car. "That will be $12.45," he said. I handed him $15 and said "thank you" as I got out of the backseat of the cab. I walk up to the large house and head up the flight of stairs. The windows are covered with blinds and curtains. I rang the doorbell and wait. Monica opens the door with a smile and said," Come on in." I go inside and hand her the cake. "Just a little something for the BBQ "I said." Oh, thank you Beth." There was no need, but the girls will love it.

Let's go sit on the back deck and you can meet everyone." Great," I said as I followed Monice outside. This is Jess, Marie, Jen, and Nick, better known as Stich. Everyone, this is my friend Beth. She has been helping me at the store and has become a dear friend. "Please to meet you," the girls said. Stitch got up and shook my hand. He is a tall slender built man with tattoos all over his neck and arms. He has a cleaned shaved face and long black hair tied in a ponytail. I smile and say, "pleased to finally meet all of you," as I sit down beside Monica. Beth will be joining us for a BBQ. She also brought a cake for dessert.

"Would you like something to drink?" asked Monica. I would love a beer if you had one. Jen, could you please go grab a beer for Beth. Sure, did you want a glass with that? No thanks. Jen came back and hands me a cold beer. "Thank you, Jen," I said with a smile. You are welcome. We chatted about anything and everything as we sit and enjoyed the sunshine. "Well, said Monica, I need to go in and get things ready for supper."" Oh, I said, let me come and help you. We stood up and went inside to the kitchen. It is a large kitchen with lots of counter space. What can I do to help? Well, how about you get the potatoes ready. Slice then and put them in tinfoil with butter, salt, and pepper." I can do that," I said with a smile. Monica gets the meat ready, and the girls help by cutting up onions and mushrooms. "I made a macaroni salad this morning and put it in the fridge," said Monica. We got everything ready, and Monica told Marie to get Nick to start the BBQ. We go outside after all the food was prepared. We will need to put the potatoes on first to get them started Monica told Nick.

After about an hour and a half, supper is finally ready. We all sit outside together at the table. It is a beautiful sunny day. A great day for a BBQ. "Where is the bathroom?" I said as I look at Jen. Oh, here, I will show you. We walk to the stairs and Jen said, "It's the door on the right when you get to the top." Thank you," Jen. I walk up the stairs and find the bathroom. I look around as quickly and quietly as I can. I take a few pictures of the bedrooms. All the window curtains and blinds are closed. The rooms have a bed and dresser in them. They all have twin beds and bright blue painted walls. I go to the bathroom and flush the toilet. I make my way downstairs to join them out on the deck. "How was supper?" Monica asked." It was great," I said. I am so full." Jess, can you grab the cake and get some plates please?" asked Monica. "Sure, "she said as she gets up. "I will help you," said Marie as she stood up. The girls came back with the cake and Monica cut it in big slices. "Who would like a piece of cake?"

All the girls took a piece and so did Nick." I am good for now. I ate too much," I said.

"Me too," said Monica. "I will have mine later." She sat down.

"Well, it's getting late and I must go now."

"Well, thank you for coming and thanks for working the store today," said Monica.

"Anytime," I said.

"See you tomorrow," said Monica. I walked to the front and left the house. I got in the cab that I had called a few minutes before leaving.

"Well," said Monica to Nick. "What did you think of her? I think she is great. She seems honest enough. If you think she is who she says she is."

"That's all that matters," he said to Monica.

"I do. I trust her with my life," Monica said to Nick. "I have a problem that I need your advice with. Beth is new to town and really needs a place to stay. Her money is running out and she can't be put on payroll in fear of being found."

"So, what are you asking?"

"Well, I thought she could come live here for a while."

"I don't have a problem if we can trust her. She will find out what goes on here eventually," he said.

"OK. Well, she will be working with me at the store whenever I need her. That can be payment for staying here."

"That's fine by me if she keeps to herself and doesn't ask questions," he said with a grin.

"Well, to be honest, I think she was in the same line of work in Toronto. She was on the streets at a younger age and taken in. She is not proud of who she is, but said she had to survive somehow."

"If you think it's OK, then I trust your judgement," said Nick.

"I do and thank you for letting me do this. It means a lot to me."

A few days went by working at the store with Monica. Everything was going well until Monica approached me and said, "We must talk." My heart fell to the floor. I thought she'd figured me out or found out I was in the cabinet snooping around. I wasn't sure what to think.

I said, "OK, what did you want to talk about?"

"Well, I really appreciate your help here at the store and I know you need a place to live. What would you think about coming to live at the house with all of us?"

"Really?" I said with excitement. "Are you serious right now?"

"Yes, I have never been more serious."

"Wow, I never expected that. I would love to. I really need a place to stay, and this would help me out just until I get on my feet."

"We can plan for you to work for me, and I will give you a place to stay and a bit of cash, as well. Does that work for you?" said Monica.

"That would work fine for me, and I can help around the house with meals and things."

"That would work for me," Monica said. "We are so busy, and meals are always so late by the time we sit to eat. The girls help as much as they can, but they get busy and forget to cook and clean.

"Today is Friday, so if you would like to gather up your things, we can have you move in tomorrow. That will give you time to check out of the place you are at."

"That would be great. I will be at your house tomorrow afternoon. Well, I work tomorrow, so how about come after supper at around seven. I will need to work tomorrow so by the time I get home and eat, it will be about seven."

"I will be there at seven sharp," I said with a huge smile, "and thank you for doing this for me."

"It is my pleasure to help a friend."

**AFTER WORKING ALL DAY,** I left the store and headed to the police van. I went inside and got a huge smile from Officer Burns. "Well, this is the icing on the cake," he said with a smile. "I am going to give you a few cameras to install somewhere in the house. You will have to just place them somewhere, so they are not seen. Like a bookshelf up high. Another good place is the top of a cupboard or hooked on a curtain. This will give us full access to what goes on inside. We will also be putting a tracking device on their van."

"I will do whatever it takes," I said.

"That's great," said Sandy. "You are doing an amazing job."

"Thanks, Sandy. I am so glad to help and get these girls out of this lifestyle." I left and headed home.

I had a great evening sitting outside and cleaning up the yard. It was so nice out and the birds were singing. I packed a few things I needed and had to make sure I didn't take too much. Officer Burns called to go over how to hook up the cameras I was given. "All you must do is put them in place and turn the little switch on the back. Just make sure they are up high, but pointed down. We will let you know once they are in place, if they are good where they are."

"Great," I said. "I will get them done as soon as I am alone in the house."

"Just watch your six. We don't want this to backfire and put you in any danger."

"I am sure this will all be fine. Monica trusts me all the way. I can tell she really needs a friend and is sure she found one."

"Well, just be careful."

"I will," I said. We both hung up the phone and I continued getting things done.

Well, it was almost time to leave and head to town. I needed to call a cab to get me to the house. I had to park my car downtown by the police van. Sandy had said they would keep an eye on it. I left the cabin and made my way to town. I stopped in the police van to leave my keys there. If they needed to move my car, then they had the keys.

"Well, good luck," they all said as I left the van.

"You got this," said Officer Burns.

"Yes," said Sandy. "You got this."

"Thanks, everyone. I called a cab and will have them meet me over toward the store." I walked and waited on the bench for the cab.

I left in the cab with a couple bags of my things. I arrived at Monica's house at 7:05. *I'm sure they will be finished eating by now*, I thought. I knocked at the door and Marie answered. "Come on in ,Beth," she said with a smile. "I hear you will be staying here for a while."

"Yes," I said. "I hope that is OK with you."

"Oh, yes. I am happy to have someone else to talk to. Let me show you to your room. It's just this way, up the stairs."

I followed Marie up the squeaky stairs and to my room on the left.

"Here you go, and I will let you get settled," she said.

"Thank you, Marie. I will put my things away and be downstairs soon." I opened the dresser and put my things in it and hung a couple of things in the closet. The room was bright but had a blind and curtains on the window. It didn't look like the window had ever been opened. Well, I would have to get it opened somehow. I needed fresh air blowing through. After about twenty minutes, I went downstairs to see everyone. It was just Marie in the kitchen doing dishes.

"Where is everyone?" I asked.

"Oh, they are out, and Monica has gone to the store to pick up a few things she needed."

"Oh, OK," I said. "Let me help you with the dishes. It's the least I can do."

"Thank you. I appreciate it."

"Where are you from, Marie?"

"Well, I was born and raised in a little town outside of Edmonton, Alberta."

"Oh, it's nice in Edmonton. I have been there years ago."

"Yes, it is but I lost my family in a house fire, so I moved around a lot. I ended up here two years ago and Monica took me in. If it wasn't for her, I would still be on the streets."

"Well, that's where I was headed if it wasn't for Monica. She is a great person," I said.

We finished up the dishes and sat in the living room on the coach. A few minutes later, Monica walked through the door. "Sorry I wasn't here when you arrived, but I needed to run out and grab a few things we needed," said Monica.

"Oh, no worries. Just visiting with Marie. She showed me to my room, and I got settled in. I didn't have much to put away," I laughed.

"That's great," said Monica. "Here, let me help you put the groceries away. I need to see where everything goes."

"Oh, thanks," said Monica. "I appreciate that." We put the groceries away and sat for a few minutes. "Marie!" yelled Monica. "Go get ready. They will be here in an hour to get you."

"OK," she said. "I will go get ready now."

Marie went upstairs and Monica went to get a shower. I was alone and ready to look for a place to put the cameras. I had a perfect spot—on top of the tall bookshelf. I grabbed a chair and climbed up to put it in place. I turned the switch on and clipped it in place. Well, that was the first one. Now to find a place for the others. The other side of the room had a tall fake plant in the corner. *This is perfect*, I thought. I climbed up on the arm of the coach and put it in place. *Two ready and one more to go*, I think. The kitchen will be a place to put one. The corner cupboard is a perfect spot to place one. I tucked it by a picture frame that was sticking out. Now all three were done. Oops, I heard someone coming. I got down off the counter and ran the water. "Oh, hi, Monica. I hope you don't mind. I'm just getting a drink of water."

"You live here now. Please make yourself at home and eat and feel free to do your thing."

"Thank you. I appreciate that."

Marie walked in the kitchen all dressed to go out. "I will be home late," she said.

"See you tomorrow," Monica said with a smile. "And be careful."

"I will," said Marie. "See you later, Beth."

"See you later, Marie."

Monica got a couple of plates and made a pot of tea. "Let's have a cup of tea and a slice of apple pie," she said.

"That would be great."

"Would you like it heated with ice cream?"

"No, just the pie the way it is will be fine, Monica." We ate and talked for hours. Nobody was home, so we both called it a night.

"I must go to work tomorrow, so I need to get some sleep," said Monica.

"It's been a long day for me, too. See you tomorrow," I said. We both walked up the stairs and went to our rooms. I stayed awake for hours. I couldn't fall asleep. It was a new place, and the bed was hard. I forgot to ask Monica about opening the window. I had no air coming in and it was hot and stuffy.

**A FEW WEEKS WENT BY,** and we were getting so much information. The tapes were in place and all the conversations were being recorded. The girls talked about their street life. The tapes showed the girls handing the money over to Nick and Monica. It was getting closer every day for making the arrests. Nobody was home, so I make a call to Officer burns. "How do things look from your end?" I asked him. Well, we are getting closer. We got so much evidence from the papers and pictures from the files you got us. We are sure there are over thirty girls that have been recruited. We also have 4 that were killed because they chose to try and leave. We need Monica to confide in you about what the girls do. We need to get her on tape telling you what goes on there. I can try to get something out of her but just need to be careful on how I approach her. She knows I know what is going on, but I haven't made any comment on anything they do. Maybe ask her if there is anything she needs help with pertaining to the girls. She may open to you about needing your help in some way. That's a good plan. I will ask her tonight when she gets home from work.

"OK, keep in touch," said Officer Burns. "And be careful."

I started to get supper ready for when everyone got home. A couple of the girls had gone out to lunch and were not back home yet. Monica called as I was getting supper ready. "Hi, I will be late getting home. Marie was hurt today, and we need to go deal with her at the hospital."

"Oh, no. Is she going to be alright?"

"I'm sure she will be, but she is hurt and in a lot of pain."

"Is there anything I can do?" I asked Monica.

"Well, just hold the fort at the house and make sure the girls eat and get ready to go to work tonight. Tell them Gordy will be picking them up at eight, sharp."

"I will and if you need me, please let me know and tell Marie I am thinking of her."

"I will," said Monica, "and I will be home later."

"I will have supper ready for you when you get here."

"Thanks," said Monica.

I wondered what had happened to her. Now I was curious and wondering who had beaten her. After about an hour, Jess and Jen came through the door carrying shopping bags. "How was your day?" they asked as they got inside.

"It was good. Looks like you two did some shopping."

"Yes, we get to shop every six months for some new clothes and things we need."

"Well, that's great," I said.

"We are going upstairs to put our things away and then we will be down."

"OK. See you in a few minutes."

I could hear the girls giggling as they made their way down the squeaky stairs. "What are you two laughing at?" I said with a chuckle.

"Oh, just at the nice outfits we bought, that's all."

"Oh, OK. Well, Monica called and asked me to tell you to eat supper and that Gordy will be picking you both up at eight sharp."

"What about Marie? Will she be here as well?"

"I'm not sure. You will have to talk to Monica when she gets home." Supper was done and the three of us sat down to eat.

"This is great chicken," said Jess.

"I second that," said Jill.

"Well, thank you, girls. It's an old family recipe that my mom use to make when I was little."

"How do you like living here?" asked Jess.

"Well, I like it so far. I don't have many friends, so this is just what I need. Monica is a wonderful person and, if it wasn't for her, I would be on the streets."

"Yes, same as all of us. We were on the streets when she rescued us and took us in. It is dangerous out there."

"Are you ever scared?"

"I get scared all the time," said Jess.

"Me too, said Jen, but we must work, or we won't have a place to live." I didn't push for any information. I just let the two of them talk so they knew they could trust me. I wanted them to be able to tell me anything.

We finished supper and the girls helped clean up the dishes. I put the supper away and the girls load the dishwasher and left to go get ready. "Thank you for supper," they said as they walked up the squeaky stairs. I yelled, "You are welcome."

Both girls came down at 7:45, ready to be picked up by Gordy. "You both look good but be careful out there."

"We try to be as careful as we can. Oh, there is the horn. Bye Beth," the girls said as they walked out and slammed the door shut behind them. I peeked out the window at the van picking them up. At 9:30, Monica walked through the door with Marie. Monica and Marie sat down on the coach. Marie had two blacks eyes and a cut lip. There was blood on her clothes and a rip in her top.

"Oh, my. Is there anything I can do?" I asked.

"Could you please get me a glass of water?" asked Marie.

"Yes, of course. Can I get you anything, Monica?"

"Yes, a tall glass of wine, please."

I went to the kitchen to get the water and the glass of wine. Marie had some nasty injuries to her face. I brought their drinks and handed them to them. "There is supper on the stove if you are hungry," I said. "Jess and Jen have gone to work."

"I will eat in a while," said Monica.

"I'm not hungry," said Marie. "I just want to get a shower and crawl into bed."

"That's a good idea," Monica said.

As Marie climbed up the squeaky stairs, I asked Monica what had happened to her.

"Well, just someone who thought they could overpower a young girl. Thankfully, she was able to get away and run for help."

"Do you have any idea who did this to her?" I asked.

"No, but the guys are on it. They have a description of the truck she got in and a full description of the guy who did this. Don't worry. This guy will be found and taken care of."

"Well, if there is anything I can do, please ask. I am here to help you guys whenever you need me to. I was a badass once or twice and I don't have a problem dealing with any situation."

"Thank you, Beth."

We sat and talked for over an hour. Monica got up and heated up supper. "This is good," she said." I think I will have seconds."

"I'm glad you like it. I am tired now, Monica, and I think I will call it a night."

"I will be right behind you. I am so tired after the day I had."

"See you in the morning," I said as I walked away to head up the stairs.

"Great, see you then."

A few days went by, and Marie was still recovering at home. Monica was still going to work, and the other girls were going out every night to work the streets. It was 7 p.m. when Monica walked through the door. "How was your day?" I asked.

"It was good but I am tired. I must go check on the girls at the other house tonight. Will you be able to stay here and make sure the girls get out the door on time?"

"I will be here, not to worry."

"That's good. Nick took care of the problem we had with Marie. It took a while, but they found him. He won't be bothering anyone anymore," said Monica.

"Oh," I said. "Well, I guess that's good news."

"Yes, Nick and the guy who helps us with the girls took care of him. They showed him what a beating looks like and then they threw him in the river."

"Well, sounds like he got what he deserved."

"Yes, and then some," said Monica. "Nobody messes with our girls."

Week after week went by and we were getting closer to close in and take this operation down for good. I spoke with Officer Burns, and he said we had enough to take them down. They would be going away for a very long time.

"When do you think this will happen?" I asked.

"We will be closing in early next week. Our plan is to get to all the girls that are put on the streets that night. We will then be able to get to the two vans at the same time and make the arrests. We will have other officers going to both houses to arrest anyone else inside. Monica will also be taken down at the same time."

"Wow, this is really happening, isn't it?"

"Yes, it is, Jill, and thank you for helping us. We couldn't have done it without your help."

"I am glad I could help. I need to see these girls off the streets and make a better life for themselves."

"Well, you do know that some of the girls will go back to the street life. That is all they know, and the money is good. When we do the take-down, we will need to arrest you, so it looks good. We don't want to blow your cover. Oh, that makes sense. "I will play along but just don't be too rough I me," I said.

A few days went by, and Officer Burns called me. "Are you able to get away today and meet with us at the police van? We are going over the take-down, which will be happening soon."

"Yes," I said. "I can be there at eleven, if that works for you."

"OK, see you then and be careful."

"Always," I said.

I was having coffee with Monica in the kitchen before she left for work. "I was wondering if I could get a ride to town today with you today when you go to work?"

"Oh, sure, Beth. Are you doing some shopping today?"

"No, well, maybe a little. I have a few things I need to get. Just a few personal items and I just need to get out for a walk and fresh air."

"I will be leaving here in twenty minutes if you could be ready to go."

"I will go get ready now."

We left the house to head to town.

"Where would you like me to drop you?" said Monica.

"Oh, the store is fine. I can walk from there."

"Will you need a ride home after?"

"No, I will go back home before you get there so I can start supper."

"You don't need to cook every night, Beth."

"I know, but it's the least I can do."

"Well, we really appreciate everything you do to help."

"I love being there and helping as much as I can. The girls are great, and we all get along so good."

I made my way to the police van to meet with Officer Burns and the rest of the team. "So here is the plan. We have everything in place for the take-down, which will be happening on Thursday. The girls will be taken off the streets the same night they get dropped off on the corners. The two vans that drop them off will also be taken down. Both houses will be surrounded, and everyone inside will be arrested, including you. We need to make this look as real as we can so there are no surprises. We will make sure Monica is in the house and the other house is also taken down. This will be a big bust. Both houses will be searched for weapons and drugs."

"Sounds good to me. It's about time for this to happen. These girls need help in so many ways."

"Yes," said Sandy. "They will get all the help they need and want. These people will be put in jail until their trial. They will be put away for a very long time. "

I left and picked up a few things and headed back to the house. The house was empty when I got back. I did a bit of snooping to see what else I could find. I made my way downstairs to do laundry. There was a door with a lock that I could never get into. I was curious to see what was in there. I looked around to see if I could find keys to open the lock. I searched a toolbox but found nothing. I looked above the door and there was a key on the ledge. As I put my hand up, the key fell. *Well, this must be it.* I tried the key and the lock opened. *Oh, this is great.* I went inside and was shocked at what I found. The room was full of guns and weapons. There were bags of drugs and money. I knew Officer Burns could see everything with the camera I was wearing. *I think we scored a mother jackpot here.* I took a few pictures with my phone and sent them to Officer Burns. I deleted them right away in case they were seen by Monica or the girls. I put the key back and locked the door. I finished my laundry and went upstairs.

A half hour later, Officer Burns called and said that was a great find. "This is just more ammunition for us to use against them." I was excited that all our hard work was soon going to pay off. These girls needed to get off the streets. I just hoped this didn't blow my cover and Monica still trusted me. After all, I would be arrested at the same time.

**THINGS SEEMED AS NORMAL** as they could be for the next few days. Today was the day of the take-down. After the girls left the houses and got dropped off in town, the police would swarm the two houses and take down the two vans. The girls would also be picked up and brought to the station. We ate supper and I made the day as normal as I could. The girls got ready to go and were picked up by the van. In the house was just Monica and me. It was 8:00 and we heard a bang at the door. This was the police. "Open the door. POLICE, OPEN THE DOOR." Monica got up and opened the door. The police stormed in and told us both to get on the ground, face down.

"Is there anyone else in the house?"

"No, no. Just the two of us," Monica said. "Beth, don't tell them anything. Ask for a lawyer."

"The rest of you go search the house."

Within a minute, we were both in handcuffs and being escorted to two different police cars. I was put in the backseat and Monica was put in another car. The police went over and told Monica they had a search warrant to search the house and property. The police car left with Monica and took her to the station. I got out of the car, and they took my handcuffs off.